A STROKE IN TIME

The story of a Newfoundland rowing record
that stood for eighty years

GERARD DORAN

For my parents, Michael and Mary Doran

Prologue

In 1977, the Outer Cove fishermen who won the 1901 championship race in the St. John's Regatta were inducted into Canada's Sports Hall of Fame:

> Walter "Watt" Power, Coxswain
>
> John Whelan, Number Six Oar, Stroke
>
> Daniel McCarthy, Number Five Oar
>
> Denis "Din" McCarthy, Number Four Oar
>
> Denis "Din" Croke, Number Three Oar
>
> John Nugent, Number Two Oar
>
> Martin Boland, Number One Oar

The course record this crew set in the championship race of 1901—nine minutes, thirteen and four-fifths of a second, the famous 9:13—lasted for eighty years. Their record was finally broken in 1981 by the Smith Stockley crew.

The members of the 1901 Outer Cove winning crew make up

seven of the nine Newfoundlanders in Canada's Sports Hall of Fame.

August 5, 1885

He dreamed, and prayed, too, that next year he would race with a crew of men, that there'd be no more rowing with the younger fellas. So many times he had pictured himself going through the final drills before the start of the race he was about to watch, the championship race. He imagined himself sitting in front of the coxswain, drifting slowly toward the start line. The crowds would be hugging the shoreline like fog to tuckamore in April and he would be in the Myrtle, *rowing with Hickey, Stack, Hanlon, and the Powers. No seat for him today, though. He stood next to Mr. Trapnell, pretending not to glance at the man's stopwatch. His heart raced, his body trembled. His eyes switched quickly back and forth from the watch to the pond as the* Myrtle *surged past the Marquee wharf.*

"Eight minutes, thirty seconds." Trapnell spoke through clenched teeth that gripped his cold pipe. He'd been so intent on the speed of the shell he'd forgotten to puff to keep the tobacco lit. "Ross's barn, nine minutes, five seconds." He raised the stopwatch. John no longer had to sneak a look at it. "It's going to be a new course record, I think."

Watt Power upped the stroke rate. The boat charged ahead even faster. Trapnell hit the stop button on his watch. "Perfection. Perfection. Three cheers for those fine rowers!" He tossed his hat into the evening sun. "Nine minutes and twenty seconds." Many more hats flew into the air.

John ran toward the finish line, trying to find her, wanting to share his elation. The champions, the Outer Cove crew, splashed each other as the crowd roared from the bank. He stopped searching for a moment and looked at the crew from the cove in the Myrtle. *Then he turned, and there was Kate.*

Chapter 1

John Whelan carefully piled the last of the fish aboard his long cart. The dried and salted cod had been placed tail to head, head to tail, over and over, layer upon layer, maximizing the load. Any heavier and Prince would struggle to haul it along the five miles of dirt road from Outer Cove to St. John's.

He tied the oilskin tarp down over the fish—almost ten quintals, he had—and stuck Prince's bulky feed bag in the only open space left in the cart. Maybe this year he would get a good price. The fish were big, and there had been little humidity when they were spread out on the flakes to dry. Less water in the salt fish meant a better price. The fish were lighter, and would last longer without spoiling. This was especially good for the markets in Brazil and Europe. The quality of the fish would not be affected by the long journey in the holds of the vessels.

The bumpy cart ride to St. John's would take about two hours. Then he would be at least another two hours at the docks, waiting in line with dozens upon dozens of other fishermen from around the shore. When all his business was taken care of and the ride home completed, it would certainly be evening. He went back into his house and told Kate he was on his way.

As he turned the horse and cart off Barnes Road onto the Lower Road, Tommy Slater, dressed in hand-me-down screeds, peered through a gap in the paling fence.

"Are you going to get a good price on your fish in St. John's, Mr. Whelan?" Tommy said. "That's a big load on the long cart."

"How do you know I'm even going to St. John's?"

Tommy wasn't finished asking questions. He raced up the hill, gaining the next opening in the fence and poking his head through it to try to get John's attention as Prince, straining, pulled the heavy load up the hill. As much as John wanted to, there was no stopping today to chat with Tommy. Getting up over Slater's Hill was hard enough with an empty cart behind Prince.

"Will you get a good price for your fish, Mr. Whelan? They says you're the best in the cove at making salt fish. Only Jim Kavanagh in Logy Bay can make fish like you."

There he goes again, thought John. *That boy knows everything.* The other boys in the cove liked to roam around the woods and swim in the Big River when they were not working or going to school, but not Tommy. He liked to spend his time with the grown-ups, and he was right inquisitive. Lonely, perhaps. The other children didn't come from a household of such misfortune.

"It's a warm day for September, Tommy. If I was you, I'd go for a swim."

"Yes, Mr. Whelan, I was thinking I'd do that. Later on, I'll go over to the river with the b'ys."

"That's right, my son. Don't go alone."

Nostrils flaring, flanks heaving and speckled with foam, Prince reached the crest of the hill without breaking stride. Beads of sweat had gathered around his muzzle. The short, steep ascent up Slater's Hill, difficult as it was, beat the other way out of the cove, that wicked, endless climb up over the Rocky Hills.

"See you tomorrow, Mr. Whelan." Tommy stopped and waved to John. He had run out of fence.

"See you tomorrow, Tommy," John shouted back.

How had Tommy and his mother survived so long in that tiny house without a husband and a father? The loss of the *Greenland* sealing steamer had made many women widows and many children orphans. The Slaters were barely getting by on a government pittance, with their few hens and the cow and a small garden. Even a small garden was a lot of work, and Mrs. Slater was a small, thin, pale woman. John shook his head. The Slaters had no relatives in the cove. Her husband had been the last Slater on Slater's Hill. Tommy was only eight, and it would be another four or five years before he was old enough to go fishing. Then he would be of some use to his mother, but only if he could endure the long days on the water and in the stages, working with the men.

Such thoughts weighed heavily on John's mind. He pushed his thoughts ahead, to the bustling harbour of St. John's, the sleeveenery of the cullers, and the aggression of the buyers. There was so much wheeling and dealing when it came to pricing the fish. The shore fish, especially in the fall, brought the best price. Naturally—it had had the best opportunity to cure.

He was past Bally Haly, now. The darkening horizon meant rain was almost certain. He wouldn't risk the steep descent of Kenna's Hill with the full load on his cart. The hill would become a slick trail if there was a cloudburst. The winding path through the meadows at Ross's farm seemed like the sensible detour. It also meant a chance to look at the pond, if for no other reason than to see that it was still there.

As he left the meadow, he halted Prince just before they entered the Cottage Farm road. He looked out at the rippling waters of Quidi Vidi. A steady breeze drifted over the pond and up the bank toward him, lifting Prince's mane. So many times he'd rowed in the wind. If only he could have had one calm day, one calm evening in a championship race. He didn't mind that he had never broken a course record. He held no grudges against the wind or the pond. It must have been in God's plan when the land was carved out that there would be people here, that they would have this lovely stretch of fresh water on the other side of the sea for their boat races. He studied the lightly ruffled pond, and was moved by memories of past victories. Were his rowing days past? Perhaps, but each race had stayed with him.

He drove on. The rain clouds raced north, and he was spared the drenching. The merging of the roads at the King's Pinch corralled the fishermen from the nearby coves and bays as they steered their loads toward the waterfront. A caravan of long carts, box carts, horses, ponies, and men jammed the rutted street with their cargoes of salt fish.

As he and Prince travelled up King's Bridge Road, John gazed upon the wealth that cod had created in the capital. Beech trees, still rich with summer foliage, towered high in the warm afternoon sun. The stately mansions of the merchants loomed over him, separated from the street by wrought-iron fences. Prince wouldn't want those fences around his enclosure. John snapped the reins and the horse pulled them up over the rise at Forest Avenue.

He had heard of the term "monopoly." Examples of

monopolies were very evident in St. John's. All trade to and from the island was controlled by a core of merchant families. The fish, the food, the sealing industry—even the nails used to build homes, barns, and stages—were in the hands of these merchants. If it took an extra dime to make things better for the merchants, the fishermen either paid that dime on their purchases or were given less for their fish. What could you do? You needed to deal with the merchant. There was no other way. A biblical quote drifted across his mind: "A merchant shall hardly keep himself from doing wrong."

He kept a close eye on the ragged children gallivanting back and forth across Duckworth Street, some with shoes, others barefoot, feet full of muck. They shouted at the men and teased the horses and ponies striding along on tired legs. They should be in school, he thought. Perhaps they were hard tickets playing hooky. He thought of Tommy Slater, safe in the little house on Slater's Hill or out roaming the good clean country.

Now he and Prince were moving past the long corridor of Cochrane Street, where coal dust dulled the painted clapboard on the middle-class homes of accountants, sea captains, clerks, and barristers. Five Tommy Slaters with gaunt faces leaned against the parked hearse in front of Carnell's. Where would their next meal come from? He frowned and looked ahead. A few more minutes to the culler at the docks.

Tommy slater pushed his way through the tree branches which were beginning to crowd the trail behind Coady's that led to the Big River. He was dripping with sweat from the afternoon sun. Was this what they called Indian summer? The crooked path, partially hidden beneath the overgrown brush, didn't slow his pace. His feet knew every dip and curve, even when the trail grew steeper on its way down to the valley. He felt his heart start to race as he got close to where the trees met the riverbank. With each step the sound of the cascading river grew louder. He stopped and pushed the alder twigs aside, and gazed down at the water plunging over Whelan's Falls into the pool. His stomach felt queasy, his head light. Slowly, he began to slide, edging himself down the rocky ledge to the river. The noise of the water increased, but the beating of his heart seemed louder than the rapids racing over the jagged granite. He was so warm. Maybe he would jump in with all his clothes on. He hesitated, then kicked off his boots. His shirt was undone except for two buttons at the bottom. He opened the shirt all the way, and tore it off. The rising mist from the water cooled him.

The sound of snapping branches travelled down the basin. Tommy looked up the river and across it. There were silhouettes of boys moving through the gnarly spruce. Their distant voices were muffled by the roar of the river. Tommy looked down into the black, foaming water. It wasn't deep, just over his head, so the b'ys said.

"I think I sees someone on the diving rock." The voices were closer now, and he could make out what they were saying. "Maybe it's Slater down there." That was Dave Houston talking.

"You're fooling. He wouldn't try that all by himself. Sure, he's afraid of the water," said Mick Burke.

"C'mon, b'ys, let's go see who it is."

Tommy knew that voice. It was Butch Devereaux. He grabbed his boots and shirt, and fled.

Ahead of him, the waterfront seemed to be a cluster of

barrels, boats, and bartering men. A fisherman never had the advantage at the trading dock. It made him feel small just to look at it, smaller still when he entered it as a peddler of fish. He just hoped for a fair price.

Murray and Sons was where he would pull up with his load today. It was the first day that the fall fish were being graded and sold. No one knew which merchant would offer the top price; the price for the season was set after the first day of selling. Pricing was complicated, perhaps deceptive. At least he would get money for his fish and then he could buy what he liked. In the outports, the merchants always had the upper hand in the dealing. There, they traded food and dry goods for fish. No money changed hands. No one knew what a sack of flour cost or what a quintal of fish was worth. It was a barter system, full of holes, twists, turns, and falsehoods.

The warm weather, the horse manure, and the fish combined made the harbourfront reek. The place had the air of a disorganized market or a carnival, with its fish and flies and the toothless hangashores who roamed the docks. Yet for all the confusion, there was a system in place to deal with the business of buying and selling salt fish. When John arrived at the start of the culler's line at Murray's, he came upon a huge pile of barrels. He wondered what their inventory of empty barrels meant.

"I don't care what they gives me for my fish," said one of the men in line. "I'm off to Boston in a month. This life is nothing but sorrow."

"Then you're in no hurry," snapped a young fellow with a Broad Cove accent.

"Move the hell out of the way, then, and let me get my load weighed first," another man shouted.

Speculation was rife: maybe there was a surplus of fish. If there was a surplus, having so many barrels made some sense. Not a good sign for prices, but it was what it was. A man didn't take his fish back to the shore if he was unhappy with the price offered. If his horse could walk the better part of a day, then he was close enough to St. John's to sell his catch. From Broad Cove, Flatrock, Torbay, even as far away as Bauline, men travelled to town in the hope of selling the year's final catch for a good price.

John liked the chance to go to town and meet other men from the coves and bays around the shore. He had worked with many of them at the front, hunting seals. They all fished from spring until September, then hoped for a berth on a sealing steamer in March month. With any luck, they'd earn enough from the hunt to scrape by until they went fishing again.

A voice rang out over the commotion. "How's she going, Whelan?"

John stared at the crowd until he spotted Mike Snow, who had made the much shorter trip from Quidi Vidi Gut.

"Hoping for the best, Snowy, that's all," John called back.

"Next! Next!" The culler grading the fish gave each fisherman a slip marked *Madeira* or *West Indies*. Luckily, there was no tal qual today. Tal qual meant that the fish would not be graded; everyone would get the same price. For the fishermen with the poorest fish, tal qual was a blessing, but for John and others it meant a lower price than they deserved. As the line inched slowly along, dozens of fishermen with their horses and ponies entered the dock area.

As he waited his turn to meet the culler, John caught a glimpse of some Torbay men. Now there was a group of hard-working men who stuck together. Torbay men sold wood, fish, and spare vegetables to the people of St. John's. Their women bought wool from the sheep farmers in Flatrock, spun it, knitted socks and sweaters, and took them to town to sell. Torbay people weren't satisfied just to make fish. If there was an extra stick of wood or any tradable commodity, they brokered it.

The culler's voice rose above the hustle and noise of the dock. "Best price for merchantable and Madeira. Best price." He took samples from the top of John's cartload, lifting the fish, smelling it, checking the texture and colour and examining it for rigidity. Then he sent John off to the weigh scales. John breathed a sigh of relief. He had hoped for a merchantable grade, and that's what he had received. Next, his load had to be weighed and unloaded. This often took considerable time. Some of the men had brought their children, but John had no son or daughter to help him at the weigh-in.

As mid-afternoon gave way to early evening, the main bulk of the sellers had met the culler and were either in line for weighing or had left the dock. Most went off to one of the many public houses in the old city for a good belt of rum. There were a handful of taverns among the clutter of buildings—Lucky Catch, the Belmont, Gosse's. The taverns opened and closed whenever they saw fit. There was no regulation in the liquor trade; it was like the salt fish system. It suited the port city full of thirsty men, including vagabonds who begged the few cents for a cup of grog or spruce beer. At least the city wasn't as crowded as it had been before the great fire less than a decade ago levelled every building from Long's Hill to Plymouth Road.

John tied Prince to a post and got him water; the horse's nostrils flared as he drank. Then the feed bag was secured around his face. John sat on the cart and watched the parade of people pass by. When Prince had finished, John took the bag and slung it on the cart, and gave some thought to his own hunger and thirst.

He had always had a liking for Scanlan's. The proprietor, John Scanlan, had both a tavern and a bond store. Each operated separately. If you had too much to drink in his establishment, he'd ask you to leave, but you could go to his store next door and buy a flask before going on your way.

John was just about to set his two feet inside Scanlan's when he saw Tom Clements, a lanky, weasel-faced scrapper from Torbay—and one of the finest bow oars ever to row on Quidi Vidi. Their eyes met, and John nodded to him before he went to the bar to break his thirst with some well-deserved ale and his fast with some penny buns and cheese.

He felt alone. Not so much because he had entered the tavern by himself, but because there was not one soul there in it whom he recognized as a friend. Also, he was sober, and it seemed that the other patrons had been there for quite some time. The place was a wall of noise, drinkers shoving and yelling, men and rough dockside women. He decided to guzzle a jar of ale, eat his cheese and buns quickly, and then escape from the boisterous crowd, the thick tobacco smoke, and the reek of sweat, fish, hops, spruce, and molasses. But as he pushed his way to the counter, Tom Clements came up beside him.

"Hello, Whelan. Did you hear that they're going to build new boats for next year's regatta?" Clements gave John a wolfish smile.

"No, I never heard that. I don't think I plan to row, anyways." He looked away, not wanting to enter into a conversation with Clements.

"What? You won't row, even if we got new boats, faster boats to race in?" Clements jeered.

John turned around. He would leave without ordering anything.

Clements stepped in his path. "Now, Whelan, stay and have a yarn with me and the rest of the b'ys. Or are ye getting too old for a few pints with us young fellas?"

Clements's buddies arrived and began to mill around him. "Some say you're no good for a stroke in the races anymore," one of them bellowed at John. Another put out his hand and tugged at John's hair, smirking. "Looks like there's a speckle of grey in that black crop of yours, Sir John."

"I can see why you want to pack it in, Whelan." Clements leaned closer. The rum on his breath made John's eyes water. But he stood his ground and let Clements spin his drunken nonsense. He looked at the bar. Scanlan was there, nodding at him. He had seen John and was holding out a drink toward him. But John couldn't reach it. The Torbay crew surrounded him. He badly wanted to leave, but he wasn't going to run away like a scalded dog.

There was a sudden tap on John's shoulder. He looked around; it was Mike Snow—Snowy. "Come on, Whelan, you'd better hop the Jesus out of this place. You're outnumbered, even with me on your side."

Scanlan came out from behind the mahogany counter and wedged himself in between John and Clements. "Now, men, this is a day for you to be toasting the sale of the fall fish, a day to be grateful for your earnings. Clements, you and the other lads from Torbay get back in your corner or you're out the door. There'll be no second warning for you." He pointed to Clements. "I'll heave you out of here, head first."

"Go back to Outer Cove and try to make a few youngsters with Kate," Clements shot at John, grinning like a devil. "She didn't mind sharing her gifts with Sammy Gosse before she met you." Then he turned abruptly and walked away, the other Torbay men at his heels.

John went after Clements with Snowy in tow. Soon the fists and the chairs and the tables were flying. But before he could get a solid shot at Clements, Scanlan had wrestled his way into the crowd and was knocking at both factions with the stout stick he kept behind the bar. John backed away. He wanted no part of the tavern anymore; Clements had almost ruined his day. He and Snowy headed for the door.

"Snowy, thanks for helping me out in there."

"No worries, Whelan, b'y. I likes a scrap myself, but they had us about three to one." He laughed. "That crowd is usually pretty decent, but they're savages today."

John's heart started racing again; he could feel the warm flush rise to his face as the blood pumped. He wasn't going back to the cove without some small reward. After saying goodbye to Snowy, he stopped in at the bond store and bought some rum. He was content that he had gotten a fair price for his fish, but upset at what had happened in Scanlan's. What was wrong with Clements? Why couldn't he just be happy with the sale of his fish and keep his mouth shut? Besides, what had Clements ever done at the regatta? Sure, he had won races, including this year's championship, but never with fast times, and always with stacked crews. Where was his record in the fishermen's race or the championship races? John would give any man his due for fishing or rowing, but he was disgusted with Clements.

His own record on Quidi Vidi stood for itself. Those who knew rowing had many times witnessed his perfectly synchronized, pendulum-like rowing form. Medium-built, broad shouldered, and with large, strong hands, he had amassed the most championship medals of any oarsman—nine in his twelve regattas. He was in so much demand from crews outside Outer Cove he sometimes, reluctantly, rowed with other crews and won with them, too. He could raise the performance in any boat.

He untied Prince, gave him more water, and then got up on the cart. They headed west on Water Street over the rough cobblestones, to Adelaide Street, and then cut over to Carter's Hill. Cracked windows and poorly hung doors creaked and banged in the brisk wind that tunnelled down the street. Peeling grey paint littered the ground. Why paint your house when there was no paint on your neighbour's?

The horse trudged along until he felt his master ease back on the reins. John got down from the cart and wrapped the reins lightly around a fencepost. Prince wasn't about to go anywhere without him. He walked along a steep and narrow street, stopped, and tapped on a door. Three young shaved heads poked their heads between the tattered curtains of the front room and then disappeared. The front door was suddenly opened by the oldest child, who said, "Mother shaved our heads because of the nits," as she elbowed her brother and sister into place behind her. They all giggled.

Their mother appeared with an old laundry basket on her hip, fit only to throw away, Kate would say. She smiled, and although her teeth were a bit crooked, the day seemed to have gotten lighter. "Jesus save me. Them youngsters will say anything." She waved her apron at the children and they disappeared inside the house. "You know, John, you can't mention a word around them." She pushed a piece of black hair away from her eyes. "My, that's some wind blowing."

"Thought you'd like a few of these." He passed the fish to her, wrapped up in a piece of newspaper. "Merchantable grade, it is."

"Thank you, John. You're a good man." She rubbed one hand over her chapped lips before she spoke. "I managed to find enough money to buy a few potatoes today. A bit of salt fish will go grand with them."

"Maggie." John nodded at her. "There's lots of fish in the sea."

"Yes, John, I knows, but I'm not a fisherman," she said, laughing. "Them children of mine, I cut their hair off so they won't catch lice. They don't have them."

"No worries, Maggie, I'm not the health inspector."

"They're the cleanest youngsters on this street." Her eyes were bright, and she laughed again. "You're heading home to Outer Cove?"

"Yes." He hung his head for a moment and then lifted it and looked her in the eyes. "I tried to have myself a drink at Scanlan's, but I had to get out of there."

"Why?"

"That's a story for another day. I got to be going. God bless you, Maggie."

He drove Prince along Queen's Road to Bond Street through manure, dogs, and children. How Kate hated this part of town. She hated the closeness of it. She pitied the people. Row upon row of houses, until there was an intersecting street. Then the same pattern of buildings all over again. No extra helping of grub on most of their dinner plates this evening. No need to save room for pudding that wouldn't be served. He snapped the reins along Prince's tired flanks. They moved slowly up Bond and then on to Military Road and King's

Bridge. The change from the centre of town to the outskirts was like the difference between war and peace.

John spent the five-mile ride from the waterfront to Savage's Bridge thinking about his confrontation with Tom Clements. The sloshing sound from the rum bottle in his pocket brought him no comfort. At last he turned down onto the Lower Road and felt a sense of calm as he observed the gentle flow of the Big River. That was where he went for brown trout and peaceful thoughts.

He stopped, got down off the cart, and led Prince to the water. He let the horse drink while he sat on the bank watching the evening sun drift toward the western horizon above O'Brien's Hill and tried to clear his mind of the many events of the day. It wasn't easy to erase all that had happened in the hours since he'd started out that morning. He thought again about Clements in the pub. It wasn't just that the man was drunk. There had to be something else. Had the younger crowd from Torbay dared Clements to confront him? The people of Outer Cove and Torbay had nothing against each other, but somehow they had no love for each other either.

John got up from the riverbank, climbed up on the cart, backed Prince away from the Big River, and turned to ride the last mile home. As he approached his house, dog tired and surly, he could smell the aroma of onions cooking with the fresh meat he had gotten from working on the Kelly farm. He got off the cart, unhitched the horse, and put him away in the barn, giving him a quick rubdown and a couple of flakes of hay. He wasn't much for hiding his emotions, and there was no masking how he felt anyway. Besides, Kate knew all the ins and outs of him. She noticed his grey mood as soon as he walked through the door.

"Well, John, there's no fish on the long cart, so it's all sold then. Can I get you a cup of tea while I finish making supper?"

He nodded. "Kate, I got the best grade, not Madeira. I got enough to settle most of the debts, and some left over. I mean, the price was good." He shrugged his shoulders. "You know, I made out fine." He stopped. Only the sizzling of the cooking meat broke the silence. "Kate." He hesitated. "I met up with that crowd from Torbay at Scanlan's after I left the docks. The crew from the north side. We had a racket."

Kate continued to chop vegetables.

"They said I'm finished as an oarsman."

"Well, John, my love," Kate said in a singsong voice, "you're closer to forty than thirty and you haven't rowed for two years." The knife chopped against the cutting board. Kate didn't look up.

"I may not row again, but I don't want to be told by another rower, especially one from Torbay, that I haven't got what it takes to row anymore."

"Ah, John, it's time to give up that rowing. How many championships have you won? Eight? Nine? What do you want with another medal? Sure, you don't even know where the ones you got are to."

John grunted.

"And there's another thing, John," she said, throwing vegetables into the steaming pot. "If you're not thinking about rowing again, and if the fishing is no good next summer, you can get work as a section man on the roads. There are things to do besides racing. Breaking your back down on that pond, that's a young man's sport."

"There'll be new boats next year, Kate. That's what they

said in Scanlan's. Torbay only thinks they're the best because they haven't had a good challenge lately."

"What do you have to prove to anyone about rowing?" With her head slightly tilted and a soft smile on her face, she said, "John, why don't you lie down there on the daybed while the stew is cooking. I knows you're not tired." Her smile grew even softer, until her eyes were like candle flames. "I might have it in me to rub your back or something, who knows?"

Chapter 2

John looked beyond the meadow out to sea. The rolling tide tossed up the white surf over the sunkers in Witty Cove. A warm breeze was sweeping through the cove, carrying the fading smells of summer. As he began to cut the second crop of hay, he spotted Tommy Slater coming toward the house.

Knapweed, which grew sporadically throughout the field, required considerable force to cut down. John gripped the handles of the scythe a little more firmly so he could cut the weed yet still maintain his cutting pace for the tall grass. Slashing away, he cleared the meadow, exposing its dark yellow bottom. Half an hour before, the grass had blown in the late summer breeze. Now it lay toppled, flattened as if the victim of a storm.

It was all about pace, whatever work he performed: hauling fishing nets, working in the garden, rowing. The swing of the scythe gave him peace. He ripped through water with the blade of an oar the same way he used the scythe on the grass. The oar slowed when it was out of the water, just like the scythe did in the air. He moved through the meadow, leaving the hay in his tracks; an imprint of his rowing in the meadow that would remain.

"Mowing the hay, are you, Mr. Whelan?" Tommy slipped through the gap in the fence and ran up to John.

He kept on mowing his hay, but he smiled at the boy. Perhaps Tommy would stay for a bit.

"I'd like to try that sometime—maybe when I'm bigger, Mr. Whelan?"

John nodded and grinned.

The lad watched him, intrigued. "How do you make the rows of hay so even?"

John stopped. "Tommy, you know, when I rows hay, I got to use a certain rhythm. That's what it takes to do the work."

"You said 'rows,' Mr. Whelan. You means 'mows,' don't you?" Tommy cocked his head.

"Did, I?" John cleared his throat. "Well, when I *mows* the hay . . ." He shuffled his feet.

"I thinks you said 'rows' because you're a rower, Mr. Whelan. My mother says you're a great rower. But she says you don't want to row no more."

John quickened the swing of the scythe. He felt a sudden rush inside him and a slight change in the rhythm of his movements. The breeze seemed to turn suddenly to a gust, distorting the calm in the meadow. He swung the scythe; the cutting was quicker and his heart raced, the same way it did when he was waiting for the call from the captain of the course; his nerves felt like they did at the start of a race. Tommy gazed up at him, uncommonly quiet. The wind moved against John's back. The sound of the slashing blade in the grass murmured between the man and the boy. The scythe dived and curved out of sight, then came back up to toss the fallen grass aside. He saw the blade of the scythe; he felt an oar. His grip on the handles tightened and his shirt stuck to his back as the sweat rolled down his neck onto his broad shoulders.

"Mr. Whelan, the McCarthy brothers are always on about

rowing in the races when they're down at the beach. Dan says he's smoother than anyone who ever touched an oar, and Denis says he's like a steamship full of power when he pulls that number four. Rhymes, it do!"

John looked at Tommy and saw the boy he'd once been. How he would stay in the field with his father, endlessly asking questions. He hesitated, trying to find a way to compliment the McCarthy brothers. "Yes, Tommy, those brothers are real characters, and, you know, damn good rowers." John smiled. "Afraid of nothing, they are. I gets a laugh out of what they says sometimes myself."

"They says they wants to get a berth at the seal hunt, and the only way to get that berth is to row for one of the merchant companies in the regatta."

John stood silently listening to the boy. "Do you believe all that talk?"

"The McCarthys says they're going to row next year. Are you going to row, Mr. Whelan?"

"Tommy, I got to keep at this hay. Why don't you drop over and see Mrs. Whelan? I thinks she's baking today." He watched Tommy speed across the meadow, jumping the newly cut rows of hay so quickly it was as though his feet never touched the stubble.

He laid the dulled scythe aside and walked stiffly to the house. His legs felt tired. A few days for drying and the hay would be ready to store in the loft.

"Is Tommy still here, Kate?"

"Yes. He came downstairs for a bit of molasses bread, then went right back up again. Flying up them stair treads like a sparrow on the wing."

"What's he doing up there?"

"It's that little model punt, John, he went up to see it. He loves it. Why don't you give it to him?"

"Yes, girl. I'll go get him. He should be getting home. His mother must be wondering where he is."

He went up to the spare bedroom. Tommy lay on the floor on his stomach, one hand under his chin, the other holding the little punt. He was moving the yellow boat around and around in circles on the wooden floor and tipping it back and forth. "Watch out," he said as he slowed the boat down. "Careful of that big wave."

"I made that punt, Tommy. Pass it up to me, my son."

John took the tiny oars from the dresser, put them in the boat, and placed it Tommy's hands. The boy looked up at him, desire and disbelief in his eyes. "It's yours to keep. You can take it to the river if you want. Just don't go near the landwash or the tide will drag it out and you'll have a boat no more." He waved Tommy down the stairs and followed him.

"I suppose we'll see you tomorrow, Tommy," said Kate. "Don't run on the way home, now. You might fall and break the little boat."

Chapter 3

"Kind of cool out tonight." Kate glanced over her shoulder, watching as John headed to the porch. "Going over to Pat Fox's?"

"Not tonight, no. I'm going a bit farther. Watt Power's."

"Middle Cove? You'll be gone a few hours." She turned up the wick on the lantern. "I suppose it will be eleven before you're back. You haven't been at Watt's house since Easter, have you?" She wiped her hands on her apron and went to him, placing her hand on his arm.

"Probably then." He buttoned up his jacket, making sure his neck was covered. "Watt should hear what Clements had to say."

"Is it him that cares, or you?"

"Kate, they were drinking, but they'll remember what was spoken." He lifted the latch. "Anyway, I'm off. I don't want to be too late getting home."

"He'll be glad to see you. Everyone loves a bit of company."

The light from the full moon was a welcome guide as he made his way along the tree-shadowed Pine Line. Traces of light squeezed between the trunks of the matchstick fir clustered along the cart path. A mouse skittered among the leaves, searching for food.

He tried to keep a clear head as he walked the final few

steps to Watt's yard. How would he get around to what he'd come for? Would Watt think he was there for some other reason? How much time would pass between the handshake at the doorstep before he felt he could start the rowing talk? As he approached Watt's house, John could see the glow of the kerosene light against the kitchen walls through the window. He knocked on the porch door, and entered.

"Hello, Whelan. What are you doing here? You lost or something?" Watt held out his hand. "Come in, b'y."

The spruce popping and burning in the pot-bellied wood stove broke the quiet of the house and eased John's mind. The flame inside the lantern rose and fell in its search for air.

"How did the fish sale go, John? I heard you got a good price."

"It went well, Watt—same as always. Big crowds around the dock." John made his way to the kitchen table and sat down. "But I had a few anxious moments after I got paid."

"What happened?" Watt raised his eyebrows.

"Oh, time enough for that. You keeping well, Watt? How old are you now?" The chair creaked beneath him.

"I'm as old as the fog, John." Watt grinned around his pipe.

"You'll soon be sixty, won't you?"

"Fifty-nine in November."

"You don't seem to be slowing down any. It must be all that good grub you're eating." They both laughed.

"Well, John, it's certainly not the number of times in the last year or so that I've put my arse in the pew to listen to Father Clarke that's keeping me in good health." Watt filled the kettle and put it on the stove. "It's one thing to preach to the masses, but to single out one person from that high and almighty perch . . ."

John nodded. He remembered the scene well enough. "Let me tell you about one recent visit I made to a parishioner," the priest had said, pausing for a moment, before going on to tell the congregation about dropping in on a certain rowing expert in Middle Cove. The expert had been discovered passed out at the kitchen table, with a rowing medal around his neck and a half-empty rum bottle in front of him. Watt had risen from his pew, left the church, and had not gone back since.

"Well, I've stayed off the grog for a year, just to keep a promise to myself that I could do it," Watt said, pointing his thumb in the direction of his chest. "You know, take the pledge." John didn't let on that he had heard all this before.

"Father Clarke and the archbishop got a promise to keep, too." Watt pointed to the picture of Jesus on the wall. "They pledged that half of what people from the cove put in the collection box on Sunday in Torbay would go toward a church in Outer Cove and we'd have our own parish." He took a pouch of tobacco out of his pocket. "I don't miss the long walk to Torbay on Sunday."

"I heard the regatta committee is building new shells for next year's races. Bob Sexton is building one for Job Brothers right now, down at his house on Colonial Street. He thinks he has the plans to make the fastest boat ever."

Watt dropped the tea into the pot. "Fast boats? That depends. Depends mostly on the crew that's in the boat. I'll tell you one thing, that crew of Roches and Kinsellas won't have any advantages in a fast boat. They have the size, I'll give them that, but they're stubborn and they don't know how to move the water away from the boat. That's what makes your boat fast and your boat first." Watt left the teapot and placed his hands flat on the table, sliding them along, one hand inching slowly ahead of the other. "You got to move the water away from the boat. Now, John, you knows a few things about that."

"What if a good crew had a chance to row that new boat of Sexton's?" John leaned forward in his chair. "Would you take them on? Be their cox?"

Watt made his way slowly to the stove and lifted the damper. The flames danced against the ceiling, casting Watt's shadow large against it. He stoked the embers and placed the damper back in place. The ticking of the clock echoed through the kitchen, interrupted only by the sound of burning wood collapsing into the stove's grate.

"Do you want to be part of that crew, John?" He cocked his head and turned toward the kitchen table. "Haven't you given up the pond? I thought you'd had enough of that racket." He took a cup and saucer out of a cupboard, poured the dark tea into the cup, and put it in front of John. A tin of milk sat on the table next to a sugar bowl. Watt got a spoon out of the drawer and placed it beside John's cup. Then he got a cup of tea for himself and sat down across from John.

"Truth is, the pond and I parted ways, but I won't part with a challenge." John slammed his fist down on the table. The cups rattled and spilled tea into saucers. "That Torbay crew, Clements and them—they got me riled. After I sold my fish at Murray's, I went to Scanlan's and they come around me and poked at me. That Clements is one mouthy bastard. I had to get out of there quick, never got a drink or nothing to eat. They were drunk, but not that drunk. Just cocky because they won the championship this year."

"Against a crew of footballers, a bunch of townies!" Watt laughed. "Nine twenty-nine in the *Glance*. Sure, I rowed faster than that in the *Myrtle* fifteen years ago."

"I'm not one to issue a challenge, but I can't ignore one either. I was thirty-six in June, but I have to row against that crowd." John folded his arms across his thick chest. "This is how I sees it. Experienced crews, they don't want a new boat. They'd rather stick to a boat they know. They don't want to spend time getting used to a boat that hasn't sat in the water before, never turned the buoys."

The wood burned slowly, turning the grate red. A sudden gust of wind raced down the chimney and shook the funnel pipe. Watt sat back in his chair and stroked his long whiskers.

"There might be a good reason to row, Watt." John shifted in his chair, signalling he was about to leave. "You knows what a good boat builder Sexton is. I think you and I should talk to him real soon. Go see him next week, maybe."

"Hah! Your run-in with Clements wasn't all bad, then. At least he told you about the new boat." Watt winked at John, and then they both rose from the table and shook hands.

"Good night, John. I'm glad you dropped over. Watch your step, now, and careful the mickaleens don't chase you going back the road. "

"Good night, Watt. Don't forget about going to see Sexton. And you best start thinking on who'll be the men to make up the rest of our crew."

John closed Watt's gate behind him and began the walk along the rocky path for home. The moon hung high in the cooling September sky, overlooking houses, barns, and fences. Everything was motionless, perfectly arranged, and at rest. Only the scuffing sound of his boots against the dirt road broke the night silence. He hoped Kate would be in bed when he arrived home, so he could watch her sleep before he slipped under the warm covers.

Chapter 4

The herring fishery was short, a mere week. Herring was an odd migratory fish. It would swim in one area of the sea for a decade, then suddenly disappear. Five cold, moneyless months lurked ahead. If the cod and herring catch were poor, a man had to be prepared to go work elsewhere for the winter. People from the cove would not take poor relief.

"Nugents have next turn at the barking pot," shouted Tommy as he ran across the beach, dodging the many boats that crowded the shore.

"Push off!" Another boat left the beach, then another, until all of them were clear of their moorings and off to the sea again. First to launch were the McCarthy brothers, Din and Dan. They stroked steadily away from shore, their legs, arms, and backs working together as they heaved the blue water aside. Their bodies were perfectly formed to row against the unyielding sea. They let the wake of the boat show those on shore their muscle.

A lone figure was standing on the grassy bank above the beach, watching the tiny boats leaving the cove.

"That can't be Watt Power," Denis grunted. "Some odd to see him around here. Must be finished his work for the day."

"Wonder how long he's been up there?" Dan grinned and

heaved the water back toward the stern. "Didn't see him until we got away from the shore." They upped the pace of the stroke rate. "Well, everyone can see him now."

They sent the boat out through the cove with perfectly pitched ash oars, their thole-pins made of black spruce, strong enough to resist the fulcrum force of the blades against the dense sea. The McCarthys were connected by birth and connected to the boat and to the water. The boat moved quickly. They were almost out of sight of the beach when Dan saw the figure of a boy walking toward Watt Power on the grassy bank.

"The beach is some busy today, so many boats. Mr. Power, do you like herring fishing?" Tommy sat down next to Watt.

"You spends a lot of time down here at the beach, Tommy. What do you notice about how the men row the boats?" Watt scratched his scruffy beard. His eyes shifted from side to side, examining every motion of every boat that raced out into the bay.

"The men who row the best, they always talks about the regatta," said Tommy, poking the ground with a piece of driftwood. "When they talks about Torbay before they heads out on the water, they makes their boats go faster. It's like they're racing."

Watt and Tommy got up and left the grassy bank, strolling together up the road away from the action on the water, away from the boats that moved against the tide, against the odds of the ocean.

It had been one week since John and Watt met, and September was vanishing along with the warm days. John tackled Prince to the carriage and set off to meet Watt at the top of Barnes Road. He knew Watt had been tempted to go on his own to see

Sexton, and he was glad Watt kept his promise about taking him along. They'd have to go in to town late in the day and wait until Sexton arrived home from his day working at the Carriage Works.

Watt slowed when they reached a long, odd-looking building that was attached to a house. "Here it is," he said. The shadows of trees hung against the timbers of Sexton's house. A crow on an overhead branch took flight, flapping its wings loudly. They were taking the risk that Sexton would make time to see them.

They heard footsteps behind them and turned and looked back along the street. A man was hurrying along it, carrying a tool box and an empty lunch basket. When the boat builder reached them, he said, "Hello, Power," and reached out and shook Watt's hand. He nodded at John. "What are you doing out this way?"

"Well . . . we're here to see the boat you're building. I mean, we heard you're building a boat and we'd like to see it, if you don't mind."

Sexton looked at Watt and then at John. He took a watch from his breast pocket and checked the time. "I don't usually let people see my works in progress, b'ys."

"Come on, Bob. I thought you were a friend." Watt looked disappointed.

"Well, all right, then. Whelan, you're no stranger to the pond either. Follow me, lads." Sexton led them past his house and into the back garden, where he had constructed the most extraordinary extension to his house for the boat. The shell was fifty feet long. He had needed a space of sixty feet in which to work, so he had built a linny onto his home. It looked strange from the outside, just six feet high, with few windows and a tin chimney pipe piercing the roof. Watt wondered what passersby thought when they looked at the odd piece of construction. Maybe they figured it was a small rope factory, an oddly arranged system of spools and coils set up without permission from the town.

The men entered the linny. Watt had never seen a racing shell under construction before. He thought of Phil Mahoney. Mahoney had built many boats, including the *Myrtle*. Watt knew every inch and curve of that legendary shell—he had rowed her swiftly to a course record in 1885. Fifteen years later the record still stood, despite a new generation of great rowers in fine boats.

"You don't think this boat will be faster than the *Myrtle*, do you?" Watt asked. "How could you build a better boat than the *Myrtle* or the *Glance*?"

"You'd need a good crew to make this one move quickly, but she will." Sexton slowly walked the length of the partially built shell. "It's the hull. Dr. Rendell designed her."

"She can't be faster than the *Myrtle*," Watt countered. "I rowed her in a light breeze to the course record. She sliced the water like a fish. Like magic."

"The man got brains to spare. I was building yachts, and Rendell's a sailor. I built him a carriage once, too." Sexton sat on a sawhorse and crossed his arms. "You know, if Rendell never had to be a doctor, he could have been an engineer or a boat builder.

"I can't read plans, so we uses hatpins to help me understand scale and distance. The pins are equal length, at ten to one, to each rib from centre board to gunwale. The ribs are an exact distance apart, to hold the planking tight to the centre board."

Sexton got up and walked the full length of one side of the half-completed boat, his hands passing tenderly over the unvarnished cedar.

"Mahoney couldn't have built this. The length of the ribs from gunwale to gunwale gives you the curve of the hull. The ribs are important. They got to be exactly the same from the bow to stern."

Watt and John had built boats themselves, trap skiffs and punts. Watt shook his head. "How do you do all this all by yourself?"

"It's not hard for me to build a boat, but I'm that much better at it since Rendell came on the scene. Dr. Rendell knows how to design a boat. Building them this way makes them faster because of the strong hull. We already knows Rendell can deliver. The last three boats I built were his design, and look at their regatta records. Look at the *Glance*! By gum, they were going to cancel the regatta in '96 if the *Glance* was entered, seeing she won thirteen out of fourteen races in '95." For a moment, Sexton's face was alive and shining with memory. Then it grew serious again. "If the hull is weak, a crew full of big men can row as hard as they want, but the boat won't hit top speed." Sexton walked over to Watt and John. "Brute force alone won't make this boat go fast. You got to know how to manage her. She'll go like the wind if you handle her right."

When he heard the word "wind," John made the sign of the Cross and looked out a window.

Sexton, eager to share his knowledge, held court for an hour or so, John and Watt hanging on his words. Darkness began to settle on the shed, and the fading evening light struggled to get through the small windows. Sexton struck a match to the wick of the kerosene lamp. Its glow pushed back the darkness in the shed, the light dancing off the hull. The long, skeletal form of the partially completed hull gave a clue to its structure.

"I never seen a boat like this before," said Watt.

"When it's finished in the spring, I'll take the back wall out of the linny before I puts the final coats of varnish on." Sexton waved his hands at the back of the shed. "I needs to be sure there's lots of warm air coming through here when the varnishing is done. It got to be coated completely in one day, and dry the same day, too." He picked up the lantern and walked along the side of the boat, holding the lantern close to the frame. "Every square inch of the hull got to have the exact same finish." He raised his hands and then lowered them as if he were taking the final details out of thin air and applying them. "If she's smooth all along the length of the hull, that will add more speed to her." Sexton patted the sleek cedar. "If a boat is exactly right—not built weak, not old and rotten—then you rowers won't have your strength wasted, strength you needs against the water. A bad shell takes the good right out of her rowers. It makes sense."

Watt looked at John and inclined his head toward the door. "It's getting late, my son. We should get back to the cove. This is fine work, Bob. Thanks for showing her to us."

John and Watt made the short, steep walk down to gather the horse and cart from the stable on Duckworth Street.

"Jeez, John, couldn't you find an easier way back to the stable than Holloway Street? This is too steep for me old knees."

"Watt, I'd say your legs are a bit weak from the surprise you got seeing that shell."

"You're half right, John. That's going to be quite the race boat when it's done." Watt grabbed John's arm as they moved toward the bottom of the street. "How will we get the use of it if we race next year?"

"Hold on, skipper, we're almost on the flat."

Though nothing was said, both men felt the temptation to turn the cart toward the Cochrane Street Hotel for a jar of ale. But John snapped the reins, and Prince kept going along Duckworth. As they travelled the worn and rattling cobblestones and rolled onto Ordnance Street, the first night stars flickered in the sky over Government House. The city had quieted down while they were at Sexton's. The night was disturbed only by the clattering hooves of Prince and the last evening run of the streetcar chugging westward along Military Road. Sparks burst from the overhead connecting rods as it passed them. Prince snorted, and John said a few soothing words to him.

The canopy of leaves overhead along King's Bridge Road dropped an early autumn leaf into the carriage, which landed between John and Watt. It had fallen silently, but it broke the hush between the two men.

"I can stroke that boat Sexton is building, Watt."

"Guaranteed, John. But it's October now. You can't plan to row next year in the hopes of finding a crew in the spring. Spring is too late, you knows that. You got to get the men to sign on now."

"Will you get the right men together?"

"I will. We'll meet on Sunday night. One thing is certain—the McCarthy brothers will row. But we needs three more besides them. I think I can find them. The hard part will be making the few fellas I won't be asking mad at me. But I'm used to that."

Excitement raced through them, and through Prince, too, it seemed, as the horse picked up his pace along King's Bridge.

"Are we going to go up Kenna's Hill, John, or down Cottage Farm Road by the pond and take the shortcut across Ross's farm?"

John smiled. He knew what Watt wanted. "We're heading to the pond, b'y."

They pulled Prince halfway down the long dirt road and looked down the bank at the pond. The absence of light did not affect its grace and beauty as it lay motionless in the quiet of the evening. How could a still, dark, mile-long length of water seem so full of life? It was devoid of motion except for the brown trout that breached its dim surface. The pond had many stories, but it was keeping them to itself tonight, those stories of victory and heartbreak—even of death.

John slipped into the quiet kitchen where Kate sat next to the crackling wood stove. He took off his jacket and cap and flopped onto the daybed.

"I'm so glad you're home. What in the name of God were you doing and what kept you so long?"

"Looking at the pond, that's all."

"Looking at the pond?'

"Yes."

"Reliving past glories or planning new ones?" Kate shook her head. She stood up, lifted one of the stove lids, and took a poker to the fire. Then she lifted a junk of wood from a box beside the stove and slipped it in. The kettle steamed to life a short time later.

"You and Watt are both fools. Old fools at that." She laughed.

"Oh, Kate, we were just looking at the pond, that's all."

"You know, there's more to life than rowing, John. Tommy

Slater was here almost till dark this evening. He said his mother is feeling sick and that she hasn't been able to care for herself or him the last few days." Kate sat down next to John and folded her arms across her breast.

"I'm sure we can find some help for them," said John, sitting up. "I'll talk to the lads at the beach tomorrow. I'll go see Father Clarke, too."

Chapter 5

Watt pitched himself on the top of the grassy bank like an eagle coming to land among her nested young. He gazed down at the boats pushing off into the choppy sea. The time to make choices for next year's crew was now. Talk and more talk never amounted to anything. Could he stay away from the drinking and build a crew? Those who work hard are rewarded. The core of the crew was Whelan—he could build around John. The others would get better by following the best.

Who would the other three be? Jack Nugent and Martin Boland were fine, experienced oarsmen. Would they want to make up next year's crew? Could they put themselves second to the crew? Could they take the hard work and the risk of everything going bust? He was far from perfect, but he could commit himself to the task. As he scanned the cluster of men in their boats, Tommy Slater appeared.

"Mr. Power, how come you don't have a boat in Outer Cove?" Tommy walked in a circle around Watt and then sat down beside him. 'You seems to like it here."

Watt hid his grin, pretending not to hear Tommy.

The boy followed Watt's stare. "Some of them men out there have rowed in the regatta, you know. They're stronger than the Torbay men." Tommy looked up at Watt. "I hears them talking. Are you too old to row anymore, Mr. Power? My mother says you sits in the boat and tells the other men how to row."

"Tommy, you're a devil for questions. But that's a fine thing, shows you're interested in how things work. You're a clever boy."

A cool autumn breeze tousled Watt and Tommy's hair. The smell of lingering wildflowers was long gone from the air, warmed now only by sporadic breaks in the clouds that eclipsed the weakening rays of the sun. Tommy stood up and leaned his elbow on Watt's shoulder, man and boy watching the men in the cove rowing out into the mackerel-blue sea.

"Mr. Power, why do some of them in the dories row together so quick while some of the others appears to be all mixed up?" Tommy moved his head from side to side. "Just look at Mr. Nugent and Mr. Boland out there. They rows like the birds. I means the geese. You knows, the ones way up high that makes that big V shape."

Watt struck a match to his pipe and made short puffs until the tobacco was lit. Tommy ducked away from the smoke wafting in his direction.

"Why do you smoke that pipe, Mr. Power?"

"It helps me figure things out sometimes." Watt smiled at Tommy. "But I don't think you should try. It might make you sick."

"Mother said if I smokes I won't grow up to be tall like a man."

"You should listen to her, my son." Watt patted Tommy on the top of his tangled mass of hair. "She's a good woman. You should always listen to your mother." Watt dusted off his pants and tapped his pipe against a rock to empty the ash.

Eager to get back to the beach and be part of the commotion on the shore, Tommy sped back down over the slope. Watt watched him jump from punt to punt, sitting down in one from time to time pretending to row or shouting from the stern like a coxswain.

Sunday afternoon in outer cove was a time of welcome rest, but Sunday evening was a dreadfully idle time, except for seven men on this particular Sunday evening. They were heading to a meeting with Watt Power at the liver house. It wasn't the grandest place to have a meeting, with its barrels of fermenting liver that stank to high heaven, but it was a private shelter nonetheless.

Watt stood at the entrance to the liver house and shook the men's hands as they arrived.

"Good evening, John."

"Good evening, Watt."

"Boland, Nugent." Watt faked a punch at Martin Boland, who quickly sidled away.

"Hello, Mr. Power," said Nugent, grinning. "The McCarthys here yet?"

"They're inside."

Jack Doran rushed up to the door, gasping for breath. "Sorry I'm late."

"Go in, we're all here now."

Watt went in last and closed the door behind him. He stood for a moment to try to gauge the mood of the room, and then he walked across the rickety floor. He checked the cover of one of the liver oil barrels to be certain it was tight before he sat on it. The stink of the place made his stomach turn. He sat down, holding his cold pipe in his hand, and cleared his throat.

"Thank you for coming this evening. I'll try not to keep you late.

"Five miles from this place is where we'll be at seven o'clock in the evening Regatta Day next year. We all know that day is our day. Or it can be." He got up and walked a few feet along the rough floorboards, stopped, then turned on his heel and returned to the barrel.

"You came here as single men—Martin, Dan, Din—" Watt pointed his finger at each man in turn, naming them, "—but we gathers here as a crew. Torbay already has their crew formed. Let's make no assumptions, but I'll tell you this." Watt paused and jabbed his finger southward, in the direction of St. John's. "When the bugle calls at the start of the championship race next regatta, the crews that answers it will be from Torbay and Outer Cove. And not one of the other Outer Cove crews, but ours. The best one."

The noise of the brook underneath the liver house crept up through the gaps in the floor.

Watt left the barrel and stepped toward the men. He stopped and looked at them. "I don't give a damn about the other crews—Blackhead, the Gut, the town crews. The whole works of them can watch the races from the shore."

"Watt, you'll have to row without me." All heads turned in Jack Doran's direction. "I didn't want to tell you that I couldn't come to the meeting. Besides, I wanted to say my piece to the whole crew. I can't row. I can't pledge to be there all the time." Doran's voice was low and thick. "Me brother Richard, he has a bad back, he can't fish all the time. And he got a young family. I got to help him out, do the work of two men. I'm sorry, b'ys."

The sound of the brook beneath the floor was suddenly

louder. The liver house had become as silent as an empty church.

"You'll have to find another number three oar. Young Denis Croke is a good hand. He's a tall lad, and strong, too. He's been helping my brother when I can't."

"You're just saying that because he's after your sister," said Dan McCarthy. "Croke isn't old enough to row with us. He's green." Dan looked at the others. "We should ask Bill Pine." He nudged Martin, who sat beside him. "He's always asking me what it's like to be in the regatta. He'd like to try it out."

"Just a minute now, Dan," said John. "I don't know where you been all summer, but I seen Croke row many times. Let me ask you this—could you row from Logy Bay to Outer Cove alone in a stiff northerly breeze with your punt loaded to the gunwales when you were nineteen?"

Jack Doran reached for the manila-rope-covered door handle and quietly stepped out of the liver house. The door closed on the remaining six. The stoggy air of the liver house seemed even thicker. Watt sensed the uneasiness. The men were thinking that perhaps a prizewinning crew was beyond their reach.

"I'm not so sure about young Croke," said Watt. "I can't say I've seen him row much."

"Then why can't you ask Pine?" Dan McCarthy wasn't going to give up on his farmer friend.

"Croke has never rowed in the races," said Nugent. "There's a big difference between rowing a trap skiff and rowing a shell on the pond. It's a big step. Most of us rowed as juveniles, and we moved up with the men as we got older. We had time to get used to the shells."

"Those shells are pretty tippy, worse if you're a greenhorn."

Din McCarthy rocked back and forth on his barrel. He winked at Watt. "If we're going after Torbay, we better be ready."

Dan jumped to his feet. "There's no bigger man in the cove than Bill Pine. I seen him building fences near our place. Three swings of the sledge and the fencepost almost disappears into the ground. He got brute strength. And I heard him say many times he'd like to row."

"Now, I'll hear nothing more of this Bill Pine on the pond in any boat that I steer. I don't have the rest of my life to teach someone how to row. He's never rowed nothing." Watt brought his hand down hard on the top of a barrel. "For the love of God, let's stop this criss-cross yapping about this one and that one."

The meeting fell silent again. Watt stood and surveyed the five sets of eyes.

"I know Pine is a strong man, but farmers don't have time to do much else in the summer but work." Watt took his pipe from his breast pocket. "Cows don't take time off. Besides, I don't think Pine ever sat in a boat before, much less rowed one."

"I seen him out in a punt a few times on a Sunday afternoon." Dan had to have the last word.

"Pine is a good man, and a hard worker," Watt said.

"Then why don't you give him a fair shot at it?" said Dan.

The stench of fermented cod livers and musty lumber wasn't as thick as the tension in the room, which was rising quicker than the sun was setting. Watt looked longingly at the door, and then replied to Dan. "I'm going to take Jack Doran's advice. I'll speak to Croke tomorrow."

"So you're not going to ask Pine." It was Jack Nugent this time.

"No," Watt said, raising his voice. "He's never rowed before. This is not a lifting competition. If strength were the only thing needed to move a boat, I'd train six oxen to row." He kicked an empty bucket, sending it tumbling over the floor. "Enough out of everybody!"

"But Croke's just nineteen," said Boland.

"Young blood can be a good thing." Watt was having trouble controlling his anger.

There was a murmur of unrest.

"Some boys are born to be at sea," John said, "and Din Croke is one of them. Croke can row and work with any of us." He went and stood beside Watt. "He's been out in a boat, sometimes six days a week from May to October, since he was fourteen. Not on the pond, but out there, out there where you become a fisherman, a rower." John kicked open the door to the liver house and pointed at the beach. "Out there, where you have to row against the wind and the waves and tides. Out there on that big pond that turns a man into a rower, a rower like me and like all of ye here." He stood in the doorway. "Croke might be just nineteen, but he's a fisherman."

Chapter 6

The liver house was empty except for John and Watt. The decision to leave Pine out in favour of Croke had been made, but Croke still had to be asked. Even if he agreed to row, he'd need a lot of practice. Watt frowned. "Well, all we can do is ask him." He drew his pipe out of his jumper pocket and lit it.

"I'll come along with you, but you can do the asking." John grinned. "After all, you're the coxswain."

"I'm sure the young fella knows who I am." Watt started pacing the floor. The fading light struggled through the dusty spiderweb over the window. "I knows his folks."

"I sees him often. I don't fish with him or his father, but he knows me," said John.

"That's fine." Blue rings of smoke rose from the pipe, almost in time with Watt's precisely placed footsteps. "We'll go together. We'll see Croke at the beach in the morning."

When they stepped out into the cool evening together, a gusty westerly smacked them in the face. Watt closed the door to the liver house and the two men headed home.

Only a fool would leave his skiff close to the shoreline when the fishing was over in the fall. Howling gales, strong tides, and winter storms ruled the deep water in Outer Cove then. Boats were no match for the big seas that launched themselves onto the beach. The stages were pitched high upon sturdy black spruce logs, which kept them safe from most rough seas, but all the boats had to be hauled up the road under the bridge, away from the wild winter water. All available men and horses were put to work getting the small boats out of harm's way.

"All hands together over here," shouted Tommy Hickey. "Let's move this punt out of the way, and get Dan Houston's big horse hooked up to his trap skiff."

"Need a hand over here to get Dan Roche's punt moved," joked Mickey Stack. "Come on, b'ys, we could lift that little thing and walk to town with her if we had a mind to."

Watt and John found themselves in a swirl of activity.

"Watt, look over there—the Crokes. When they starts to haul their boats, we goes over," whispered John.

The clanging sound of the horses' shoes and the slapping of the men's boots on the beach rocks complemented the bustle on the beach.

"There he goes, with his father," said John to Watt. The two men lowered their heads and walked toward the Crokes, pretending to be heading home.

The Crokes and the Smarts were putting fir logs in a boat's path to help it roll over the rocks. Watt and John joined them.

"Four on each side, then, haul! Haul!" There was a roar as the skiff slid along the logs toward the bridge.

"Thank you, John. Thank you, Watt. Glad you came by. Can always use an extra hand at this racket," said Will Croke.

John and Watt sat down on Croke's overturned skiff.

"You've spent a lot of time rowing this big boat, Din," Watt began.

"Oh, yes, and many times it was full of fish, too," Croke said, laughing.

"Did you ever think about rowing on Quidi Vidi?" Watt put the pipe in his mouth. "You know, give the races a try. I'm looking for a man your size and age to go after the championship next year."

Croke sat on the gunwale of a nearby boat and looked out toward the expanse of blue horizon.

"Mr. Power, would the McCarthy brothers be part of your crew?"

"Yes, my son. Martin Boland and Jack Nugent, too."

Croke was silent for a moment. The gusting breeze sent his hair flying across his striking blue eyes. "Why should I row? Don't you suffer like a martyr in the races? What's in it for me?"

Watt walked away from the young man, then slowly turned back to face him. "Honour for the cove, and honour for you if we wins. There's some prize money, too, if we break the course record."

"And if we don't win?"

"We'll train to win. We'll train so hard the racing will come easy." Watt went back and stood next to John and relit his pipe.

Croke grinned. "If I joins up, who will be the sixth rower?" His eyes shifted from Watt back to John.

Watt gave him a half-smile and tilted his head toward Whelan. "John will be the sixth man. He's stroke oar."

Croke reached out and grasped Watt's hand. "Mr. Power, I would be honoured to row for Outer Cove."

The November sun broke out from behind the clouds, briefly lighting up the boats, beach, and men.

* * * * *

John knew that the blisters on hands and backsides were not the only painful parts of rowing. The people were an even more difficult aspect of the sport—the people in the boat and the people in the crowd on Regatta Day watching the boat. Both had expectations. The meeting at the liver house had been the first small step in the process of making a tight crew. Watt had a long way to go before that process was finished.

The months leading up to the first practice on the lake were often clouded with doubt. Everything was a gamble. Everything rode on one calculated bet, full of risks: bad weather, a broken oar. People quit, too. "My son, if you can't take the strain, don't row." That's what John's father had told him. Still, even with his own headwinds to battle, he couldn't stay away from the pond. His thirty-six years and his fifteen regattas seemed like two lifetimes. Would he live up to the hopes of the crew and the cove? Was he hanging on too long to the sport he had mastered? Self-doubt had inched its way into his soul.

If he had moved to Boston or New York, like so many others, would that have severed the cord that bound him to rowing? Perhaps, but he hadn't moved. He had stayed in the cove. He had never seriously contemplated leaving. His connections to the place were too strong. The sea, Kate, his good friend Watt, they were all part of his constellation in the cove, his world. If life changed, perhaps he would move on. Move clear of the pond. Move clear of that time. For now, at least, he could not untangle himself, mind or heart, from the rowing. He couldn't walk away.

Not yet.

He was not a young man now, but he could still fell the hay in the meadow at the same rate as in summers past. He could go into the woods with a bucksaw for a day in the dead of winter and work and work. Maybe he was beginning to spend too much time thinking about his age, his life. He could see how some people slowed down with time. He couldn't recall not being able to work at the pace he did yesterday, last year, or five years ago. Perhaps soon his muscles would begin to soften, his speed decline. Seven months from now, would he be able to hold up for one more mile and a half on the pond? He just wanted one more race, one more Regatta Day to do battle.

    He tossed in the bed, slipping in and out of short moments of restless sleep, wishing morning would come. A tiny ray of moonlight broke through the clouds and slid past the curtains, fading into the colourful rug Kate had made last winter. He couldn't stop thinking, turning again and again on the soft feather mattress, trying not to disturb Kate, closing his eyes and drifting toward sleep, but not reaching it. Count the strokes in the water. Count sheep. His heart was beating too strongly to let him rest. He changed his position again, put his face down in the pillow. Full darkness. He thought of Clements and felt his fist clench. It was not good to hate. He knew that through Christ. He started to count again, the sweeps of the scythe in the meadow this time. At, last he drifted off.

Chapter 7

Mary Nugent was tired of looking out the window. She sighed, peeled the bread dough from her hands, and pushed her knuckles back into the ball. This would be the second batch today.

Jack suddenly appeared from behind the root cellar and slowing began angling toward the house. Mary continued to manoeuvre her fingers in the dough, her hands now fists that pulverized and flattened the mix. She rolled, turned, and squeezed the dough. Her heart thumped as Jack got closer to the house. The latch rattled and the door opened, letting the cool fall wind rush into the warm kitchen.

"Jack, you knows I heard about the meeting at the liver house on Sunday night."

"But, Mary, I—"

"Jack, shut your mouth." She felt a lump in her throat. "I can't understand why you would go there without telling me." She tried to swallow to clear her voice, but it only made her eyes water. "You promised you'd tell me if you were asked to row again." She turned away from him and looked out the window. The fog was rolling over the bog and disappearing into the tall stands of juniper along its edge.

"I believe I'm pregnant, Jack." She tilted her head and

sniffed back the tears. "You can't row this year. It's a young man's sport."

"My God, Mary, not another youngster." He bowed his head, then raised it again and gave her an awkward pat on the arm. "I'm sorry, my love. We're young yet, Mary, don't be bawling."

Mary looked at the cradle and raised her fingers to her lips. But it was too late. The baby cried out. She walked over, bent down, picked up the bundle of unhappy sounds, and soothed it against her shoulder.

"I can row one more year. I can carry the load for you and the children. Rowing in the regatta means a lot to the people in this cove. It means a lot to me. I wants to show those townies what good rowers we are. They thinks we're only good for hauling fish and getting on the rum."

"Jack, I knows you're not old, and you're still strong, but you have five mouths to feed. Six, come the summer."

"Mary, I'm twenty-seven." He turned away from her. "Of course I'm not old, for Christ's sake." He grabbed his thick black hair with both hands, as if he was about to pull it out. "I don't know who I can't stand more, the townies or Neddy Gosse and that crew from Torbay." He sat down at the table and placed his head in his hands.

The bread dough, uncovered and cooling, began to fall. Mary put the baby back in its cradle and began to revive the dough, her hands kneading rapidly, her tears falling into the bowl.

Jack got up and went to her, putting his arms around her waist.

She pulled away. "Jack, there's another thing," she said. "I does a lot of work at the fish. Do you want me to catch them, too? Rowing! What is it with you men and the rowing?" Choking on her tears, she yanked off her apron, threw it over the bowl, and hurried away into the front room. Her husband followed.

"Mary, I can't tell you why I want to row. You'd have to row yourself to know. Sure, sometimes it's harder work than fishing. But I got to do it, for the cove. And for myself. One thing for myself, Mary, is that too much to ask?"

She stared out the window. The fog was still rolling in across the bog. It looked as though it would keep rolling until the Day of Judgment. "Don't you get enough of hard work trying to make a living and raise a family? First it's the salmon, then the cod in June and July. Trawl fishing in September, October. You never stops rowing."

"Mary, it's different this time. We have a great crew."

"Jack, I don't care if it's God Almighty steering the boat. I don't want you to row." She dried her eyes with the yoke of her dress. "Where are you going to get the time, when you're out of bed at four in the morning going to the traps? In the evening, I suppose, like always—off to the pond to practise." She shook her head. "Jack, Jack," she said. Her face was red where she had wiped it with the coarse material. "Jack, tell me what's different this time. Is there something different for me? What about some help for me with the children? Or is it just different for you? Yes, that's it, it's only different for you." She brushed away a long black hair that was sticking to her cheek. "Tell me to my face now that you won't ever row again after next year—never again. You made your decision to row, I can see that, and you broke your promise to me. God help me." She covered her face with her hands and fell down heavily on the old black couch. Its horsehair pricked the backs of her thighs through the worn dress. "Our folks are getting old, we have a young family, animals, a garden. All them things got to be cared for." The last words were barely audible; her voice had given up, too.

Jack looked blankly at the floor.

Mary's voice was on the mend. The first words were low and hesitant, but the last ones sounded like they came from her usual self. "Now tell me, Jack. What will be so different for you next year?"

"Mary, I just could not say no. I didn't row this year, and I thought, perhaps, after a year away from rowing, I could go back and you wouldn't make such a fuss. I'm still young. I can't row when I'm dead." He turned and started to walk toward the kitchen, then turned back to face her. "Watt Power called on me. This will be a great crew, the best crew. I could not say no. He asked me to go with these men, to go with these men for the cove."

Mary sighed and looked at the ceiling. A pale stain was making its way across the plaster.

"We nearly never had a crew. Some of them wanted Bill Pine to row, but Watt refused to take him. He fixed on young Din Croke." Jack walked back into the room and sat down beside his wife. Her tears seemed to have dried. He took her hand and squeezed it, and after a moment or two she returned the gesture. They held each other's hands carefully.

"Jack," she said, pulling him close, her voice sure again, no more quiet broken words, "sometimes I wish you were a farmer like Bill Pine."

He kissed her face.

Chapter 8

Kate was worried about Agnes Slater. She gazed through the kitchen window at Agnes's distant home as she placed the damper back on the stove and readied John's morning meal. It had been three days since Agnes had last been outside her house.

"My son, I thought you'd never wake up!" Kate tossed one piece of dough after another into the hot frying pan until it was full. Salty vapour hung in the house like bog mist.

The pork fat crisping with the dough stirred John's appetite. He took the boiling kettle off the stove, put tea in the pot, and poured the hot water in. He kissed his wife on the cheek.

Kate turned over the toutons. They were a fine shade of brown. "What happened at the liver house?"

"It looks like we have a fine crew, but there'll be a lot of strokes between now and the time the regatta comes around next August. I'm sure we have the right men, all the same."

"John, I hope you got that message about Agnes to Father Clarke. I haven't seen or heard a peep from Tommy in two days. Though, I suppose that's not odd, considering there's not much going on at the beach." She shook her head as she took the food from the pan. "Between all the work and all the storytelling that goes on down to the beach, that boy is stuck there like maggots to a rotting fish."

"Do you think Tommy would tell us if his mother was worse?"

"He's just a youngster. He probably wouldn't notice." Kate placed the plates on the table and sat down. She picked up a fork and looked at her husband. "I'm right concerned about her, though. I brought some fresh bread and soup to her and Tommy a few days ago. She sat up in bed and ate a little, but she was miserable. I think she needs more than Father Clarke's prayers and blessings."

John ate the delicious hot food, not taking his eyes off her.

"Well, did you get the message to the priest or not?"

"Kate, Kate, of course I did."

"You had your rowing meeting. Is that more important than a sick woman with a half-orphan child? Are you going over to Torbay to bring Father Clarke to the cove or am I going to do it?"

John sipped his hot tea, trying to shake off the last remnants of his deep sleep.

"Don't be fussing, Kate. Father Clarke is going to see her today. He promised me he would. He said if he thinks she's bad off, he'll get a doctor to the cove. Sure, he'd know whether she was bad off or not, he's seen hundreds of sick people."

"You had better go to Torbay and make sure he comes over. I'm telling you, John, go. Whatever you got planned for today, you can put it aside." Her voice sounded like a gull's, high and keening.

"What are you saying, Kate? That Father Clarke is not a man of his word? Stop fretting, woman, he'll come." He turned away, mumbling.

"Don't call me woman. Go tackle Prince up, or I'll do it myself."

John kept quiet. His throat felt queer. He couldn't look at his wife.

"Do you care at all about the child, John? He's around this house often enough. If she's taken bad, what will happen to Tommy?" Kate opened the porch door and looked in the direction of the Slater home. "He did have an aunt in town. But I don't know nothing about that, where she lives, if she's married."

"Now, Kate, he's not our son."

"They're our neighbours, John."

"Father Clarke will see to it that he's cared for. They have homes for orphans."

"Homes? The child don't want homes, he wants one home. Anyway, what's the use of speculating about Tommy and his mother? We're not prophets nor gypsies. We can't predict the future, and we shouldn't try."

Kate rapped again on the unpainted porch door. A faint puff of smoke rose from the rock chimney and was flattened for a moment to the rooftop by a stray breeze before skittering away. The smoke was more blue than grey, the kind that would burn your eyes if you stood too close to it. She knocked one more time, and then listened hard at the door.

After lifting the latch and opening the door, she stepped inside the musty porch. An empty coal bucket lay on its side. A ragged man's jumper hung from a rickety dowel rack. It was if the house had been abandoned. She felt something unpleasantly soft under her shoe, gathered up her skirts, and reached down to remove it. Raising her hand to her nose, she discovered that the porch was also a roost for the Slaters' hens.

She tapped on the kitchen door once, a second time, a

third time. No answer. Two people should be in there, she thought. What was happening in this house? She placed her hand on the doorknob and turned it gently.

"Hello? Hello, Tommy? It's me, Mrs. Whelan. I thought maybe you'd like to come up to the house for a bit. Hello, hello? Agnes?"

She opened the door and went into the chilly kitchen. A weak voice whimpered in a room at the back of the house.

"Are you still in bed, Agnes?"

Kate's heart raced as another whimper echoed through the damp, bare house. She crossed the unswept floor, stepping over rags and scattered wood ash and wrinkling her nose at the stink of the slop pail. Another sound came from the back room.

"Agnes, it's me, Kate Whelan."

The foul smell of infected urine and worse met her as she went along the narrow hall from the kitchen to the bedroom. She stuck her head into the open bedroom doorway. Tommy was there.

"She's cold, and I'm keeping her warm." He was lying on top of the covers, clutching his mother. "She kept saying she was cold, so I laid next to her, but now she's even colder." His face was white and tear-stained. She had to strain to hear him.

Kate walked to the bed, her heartbeat in her ear louder than her footsteps. She looked at Agnes Slater. The woman's face was as pale as an altar candle and there was no sign of movement.

"Yes, Tommy, I can see your Mammy is very cold." She edged onto the bed and gently stroked Tommy's head. She placed the index and middle fingers of her other hand on the woman's cool neck. The vein carried no pulse, not the smallest throb of life. She moved her hand over Agnes's mouth. There was not a trace of breath.

"Tommy, come away home with me and I'll fix you something hot to eat. John's gone for the doctor. Let your mother rest until he comes."

Father Clarke would not have to come over from Torbay today. John would be tackling Prince up to the carriage for a trip to town. Dr. Donahue would come to the cove to verify Agnes Slater's departure, and inscribe her name on a certificate of death.

Chapter 9

The surging sea foamed and rumbled at the shore. As the waves receded, they hissed along the landwash, sending salt air drifting up into the cove. In the Whelan home, steam from the cooking dinner made the kitchen windows opaque, creating a shroud of privacy.

Christmas morning brought all homes in the cove a much-anticipated day of tranquility. It was as if some almighty peace bore down upon the land and sea, imposing an unshakable calm. No sounds. No cartwheels turning. No feet walking on the snowy roads. Even the farm animals seemed to sense the grace of the season.

Tommy came swiftly down the stairs with messed-up hair and eyes like a preying owl. He stopped at the entrance to the kitchen. Kate was getting ready to go out and feed the hens. John was sitting at the table drinking tea.

"Why are you stopping?" asked Kate. "Keep coming."

Tommy had stopped because he was afraid that the big woollen stocking of John's he'd hung by the stove would be as empty as it was last night. He gathered up his courage and went into the kitchen. He forced himself to look at the stocking. It was round now, and bulging. He felt a sudden pain in his stomach, the result of a mix of joy and relief. Kate came and led him by the hand to the pantry. On its floor was a large brown paper package neatly tied with string. He heard John's voice.

"Thomas, my son, we thought you'd never wake up." John laughed. "Come on, go ahead and see what's inside."

Tommy dropped to his knees and touched the package. He tried to lift it and grunted.

"Tear away the paper. See what it is." Kate's voice was high, excited.

"It's not for lifting, Tommy." John came around Kate and knelt beside Tommy.

He broke the string and began to rip the paper away, uncovering solid wood painted red. When the paper was all torn away, Tommy was looking at a brand new slide. Without a word, he turned to John, his hands dangling at his sides. His face was crumpled; he looked as though he was about to cry. John, worried, clapped him on the shoulder.

"A slide, b'y, a new slide. Made it for you meself. Don't you like it? Come on, now, get up and we'll take her for a run."

"First he got to see what's in his stocking." Kate reached down and plucked the boy off the floor. "I told you Santa knew you moved house, Tommy."

"Let me go, let me go." Tommy wiggled away from Kate. "I got to sit on it."

"Go on, now, scatter and get ready. Take her for a run down Slater's Hill. Don't get hurt. Dinner will be ready in a couple of hours."

They could hear Tommy's feet drumming on the stairs.

Kate turned to John and smiled as if she had gotten a gift instead of Tommy. *She has, too,* thought her husband. *A gift I couldn't give her.* A youngster to love and to fuss over.

Tommy grinned. "i'm gut-foundered, aunt Kate." The smell of the roast chicken, flavoured by savoury and onions in the bread stuffing, was making his mouth water. Bowls full of vegetables from the garden surrounded the platter.

"Before we begins, we will give thanks for this fine feed of grub," said John. He bowed his head. "Bless us, O Lord, and these Thy gifts, which we are about to receive from Thy bounty, through Christ Our Lord."

Tommy made the sign of the Cross and began to eat.

They cleaned their plates. Kate served a second helping, and that, too, was quickly eaten.

"Not many in the world with a feast like this," John said proudly as they finished their meal.

"If I keeps eating like I done today, I'll be the strongest man in the boat someday," said Tommy.

Kate looked at John and then Tommy. Her husband reached over and touched her cheek.

"There are many things that make a good man," said John. "A good wife is one of them. And another is a fine lad to take fishing someday."

"Can I go sliding with the Stacks and Roches later?"

"Yes, me son. You can go at it till dark."

Their bellies full, the heat from the kitchen stove shifted them into a lazy, napping state of comfort. Tommy, content with the Christmas dinner that ended with Kate's fruitcake, crawled onto the daybed and rested his chin on the windowsill. He drew pictures of boats on the steam-covered glass. John slipped onto the daybed beside the child, where he soon sank down into slumber.

"Ah, my God, I'm tired." Kate yawned as she placed the clean dishes in the cupboard. She didn't expect a response. The quiet from outside had slipped into the Whelan home. The hissing of the burning chunks of spruce was the only sound in the kitchen. She decided to go upstairs for a lie-down.

"There's someone coming in at the door." Tommy poked at John with a thin finger.

"Christ," John said. "I was that deep into my nap I don't think I could have dreamed if I tried. Hardly know where I am, my son. What are you on about?"

"I think it's Mr. Power. I hears him hollering. Mr. Power from Middle Cove."

"Hello, Mr. Power. Happy Christmas to you," Tommy said to Watt as he entered the kitchen in his stocking feet, his battered old boots behind him in the porch.

"A happy Christmas to you, young Thomas," Watt replied.

John got up from the daybed, stretched, and grinned at Watt. "Watt, you old devil, destroying a man's nap on Christmas Day. Have a seat. Take up a plate of grub first, you looks half-famished."

"No, b'y, no grub. I'm as full as an egg. Just came from my sister's. B'ys oh b'ys, some scoff she had on."

"Can I get you a drop of the stuff?" asked John. Watt nodded and sat down, and John placed a tumbler in front of him.

"Just a drop. First taste in many months."

John nodded and poured Watt a finger of dark rum. "Not on the pledge anymore?" John said, grinning.

"You know, John, I don't miss the drink one bit. I thinks I could just as well not have a swalley ever again. Only having this one because it's Christmas, but I'm not one bit tempted. You can tell that to Father Clarke."

John laughed and poured himself a generous tot.

Watt smiled, licked his lips, and raised his glass. He and John both shivered a little as the Jamaican liquor sent a warm rush through their bodies.

"I'm hearing a rumour about the McCarthy boys," Watt said.

"What is that, now?" John tapped his fingers in a rhythmic pattern, starting with his pinky and ending with his thumb. "I saw Dan a few days ago in town. He never said nothing to me."

"Well, b'y, I can't say for sure," Watt said, "but it seems that they both got a good chance to go to the seal hunt this year with Baine Johnston."

"And what's wrong with that? I'd go meself if I could get a goddamn berth with them or any other decent sealing crew. Seems like if you're from the cove and your name isn't Kinsella or Roche, you can't get a spot on a vessel. Sure, and that crowd hasn't won a regatta championship for years. Boils my blood." John slammed the tumbler down on the table. "I don't begrudge them a trip to the ice. Everyone knows they've been getting the trip to the front for the rowing they did for Job and Murray and Sons in the regatta. I gave up trying to get a berth. Not worth the trouble."

Watt looked silently at John for a moment. Then he spoke. "You're getting the idea, John. You're onto it. That's what the McCarthys have in mind. Get the berth with Baine Johnston by rowing with their crew in the regatta. Or the Feildians, bunch of goddamn Protestants. Bill Pine told me that an offer has been made to the lads. Bill wouldn't be codding me, neither. Now, there might be some confusion as to what's in the works, but something's going on with them two, Din and Dan. We got to get to the bottom of it right away. The boys didn't have a great year fishing. You knows that story. They'll be glad to get a berth to the hunt with anyone. I don't know, John. We might be in a bit of a bind." Watt took out his pipe and lit it.

"If this is true, our crew is ruined," John said. "Where would we get two good experienced hands like them?"

"It's what I hear."

"The devil is making his way into them fellas' minds. There's an Antichrist at work somewhere. Come on, Watt, we're going up to McCarthys' now. I won't have no peace this Christmas unless we do."

Tommy looked up at John, his mouth open. John rubbed his head and smiled at him. "Never mind, Thomas. It's only grown-up foolishness." He felt cold. The drink he'd shared with Watt no longer warmed his blood or spirit.

Kate's footsteps sounded on the stairs.

"Hello, Watt. Couldn't wait until St. Stephen's Day for your Christmas visit, could you, b'y?" She smiled at him and then shifted her eyes in Tommy's direction.

"No, Kate. Besides, I needed a long walk after all that roast beef. Mr. Kelly slaughtered an old cow last week and gave us a cut of it. The meat was a bit tough, but it tasted best kind. Kitty is a grand cook, and she bakes to beat the band, too."

"Watt, your sister got you spoiled. I suppose you and John are having a talk about the rowing. I wouldn't be completely wrong about that, now, would I?"

"Oh, you're spot on, Kate. John and I were discussing this and that. Being the races are only seven months away."

"Come on, Tommy, I shows you the nice storybook Father Clarke gave you for Christmas." Kate turned to Watt and dropped her voice. "Father Clarke gave it to me after his mother was buried. We kept it aside for Christmas." She reached out and took Tommy by the hand and made her way out of the kitchen. The boy went along as if he'd been with her since the day he first walked.

"Well, it may only be talk," John said, "but there's got to be a story behind it. Maybe it's just an offer. Maybe a tease to see if a trip to the hunt is something the boys will consider. I can't understand for the life of me how the seal hunt and the rowing are connected."

"It happens more now than it used to," said Watt. "Companies wants to get their names associated with the winning crews. Can't say I blames them. Make themselves look good while they're gypping us out of a decent price for fish and sticking men in the hold of them filthy sealing steamers."

"I'm still fuming over what that Torbay crowd said to me in Scanlan's in September."

John clenched his teeth. "Like a crowd of wolves, they were. Let's go up to McCarthys' now. To hell with it. I don't care if it is Christmas Day."

"We can't go there in this mood. And we shouldn't jump to conclusions or start a racket yet. Who knows what the truth is? Tomorrow is St. Stephen's Day. Everyone will be moving around the cove, mummering and the like. Why don't we pay the boys a visit tomorrow, early in the day, before they gets on the move?

"Let's enjoy our last mouthful of rum," Watt said. "Tomorrow we'll go to the McCarthys'. Unless Bill Pine got it spread all over about the boys and their sealing plans, there's no need to get too worried yet."

"Not yet, Watt." John laid a heavy emphasis on the second word. "Bottoms up." They clinked their glasses, downed the rum, and got up from the table.

Chapter 10

"A happy Christmas to you, Mrs. McCarthy." Ellen McCarthy turned around, wiped her hands on her long apron, and smiled at John and Watt. She waved them past the doorway of her large kitchen, which was full of fragrant heat from the baking.

"Come in, come in! Oh, we'll have the rowing talk today with Power and Whelan here. The boys are around somewhere, Watt and John.

"Dan! Din!" she called. "Your rowing buddies are here. Well, your buddy John Whelan is here. I don't know about Mr. Power—hard to call him your buddy when he makes you work like dogs on that pond." She laughed. "Just codding, Watt. You're the finest kind of a man and a grand coxswain.

"Everyone in the cove knows you're after putting together a dandy crew, and they're all delighted. You knows we starts looking forward to going to the races long before August. Now, if the boys would only come out of their rooms. I'll go give them a shake."

"Dan's in Logy Bay, Mother." Din's voice came from one of the back rooms.

"That Dan and Liz Malone. I've never seen the sky so clear above a young couple. I suppose he'll be married to her next year, if he doesn't crack up beforehand with his first romance." She laughed. "Oh, me nerves! Come out, Din. John and Watt haven't got all day to wait on you. Sit down, I gets the two of ye a cup of tea and some of them biscuits I'm just after making."

Din ducked to clear his head of the door frame as he entered the kitchen. Watching him, John thought that if his shoulders were any wider he'd probably have to turn sideways to make it through the opening. Their father had been broad-shouldered and rugged. Built like a bear. His sons were the same shape, but taller. John looked at their mother and wondered where she had gotten the strength to bear and rear two such sons. She was like a sparrow, and just as lively.

"Hello, John, Watt." Din shook their hands. "The very best of the season to you both."

"Are you still courting Sara Fitzgerald?" Watt asked. He didn't want to jump into the rowing right away. Before he came out, he'd lined up his words like horse carts at Haymarket Square.

"Yes, sir. Two years now. If I gets a good spring at the seal hunt and a better summer at the fish, we'll marry in the fall."

"If you gets a good spring at the seal hunt," Watt said, raising his eyebrows. "Might want to get a berth first, don't you think?" It was hard not to spring another question on Din. Watt felt the pressure mounting, and wondered if Din sensed it, too. Before he could say another word, Din cut in.

"Looks like Dan and myself may already have a berth. It's not for certain yet, but it seems likely if we agrees to . . ." He paused and began to walk around the kitchen, peering about like a crow guarding its meal.

"I wants to tell you something. Dan should be here to talk about this, too." Din glanced toward the stairs. "Never mind. It don't matter if Dan is here or not." His stocking feet were silent on the bare wooden floor as he turned. "We don't know if we can row with ye next year."

Watt hadn't expected to hear him confess so quickly. The room was quiet as the grave. Ellen turned away from the stove to look at her son.

"Baine Johnston added another ship to their sealing fleet for the spring hunt." His words were hurried. "We happened to find out last week that they needed to crew the new ship. Dan and I went straight to their office in Ayres Cove."

"Why didn't you tell us?" Watt's eyes shifted toward John. "We're all part of this crew, this plan to bring a championship to the parish. Well, a parish in the making if Father Clarke lives up to his promise. Maybe promises and handshakes don't mean nothing these days." Watt folded his arms across his chest and tilted his chin.

"I should have told you sooner." Din's voice quivered. "Let me tell you the pure and simple truth, which is not easy."

"Let me tell you something, McCarthy, and it's damn easy." John's voice cut the air like an oar. "God forgive me, but where is your loyalty to our crew and the people of the cove? We all have to work hard, make a few dollars to try to get by. We understand that. So why the hell are you and your brother not showing the rest of us some courtesy?"

"For Christ's sake, John." Din's voice was sure and steady now. "What do you have to lose, anyway? You got lots of wins on the pond, lots of medals. You can row with any crew and likely win. If you don't row, it won't matter a pound of salt fish. That's two and half Jesus cents."

Ellen was staring out the kitchen window, her back rigid. John glanced at Watt.

"Din," Watt said. "If Baine Johnston is adding another ship to their fleet, it might mean they're hoping for a better market and prices for next year's pelts. One thing's for sure, they're not going to tell anyone that. Maybe the other companies plan to add more ships and men, too. Why trade off your chance of a berth at the hunt along with your rights to row with whoever you wants to?"

"Watt, they're going to give us a berth. It's not that easy to get on with another crew. The whole damn island wants a berth on the sealing ships." Din pounded his fist on the table and rattled the whole kitchen. "You knows how it is with the outharbour men. No cash at all. It's some cursed system we lives with, but they got it worse. Call it what you like, but when you goes to the hunt and you hits the big patch, you gets cash in your hand afterwards and you can thumb your nose at the merchants then, buy what you likes.

"I wants to row, I do. I wants to eat, too. Have a bit of extra money. Maybe earn enough to start building a house in the fall. I've been to the hunt. I knows what you got to put up with. There's no promise that seals will be found. Ships get stuck in the ice and some come back with empty holds."

"My son, you don't have to sign to any company right away. Will you and Dan give another company some thought? You're good hands at the swiling. Baine Johnston or any other outfit isn't going to take a bunch of half-starved corner boys. The seal hunt is three months away. If you hooks onto another crew before the hunt opens, Baine Johnston won't have any trouble finding replacements for you and Dan. That's a guarantee."

Din felt like he was trying to stay level in a heaving boat on a stormy sea. Christmas was off to a rocky start, and St. Stephen's Day had not lived up to its reputation for cordial and neighbourly visits. Why the Christ did Dan have to say anything to Bill Pine? And why did Pine have to shoot off his mouth to Watt? Maybe he was trying to make trouble because he hadn't been picked to row. Din felt like he was about to dissolve in the heat of the kitchen and the heat of the words between him and Power and Whelan. Rowing was torture, on your muscles and on your head, pressing against all of your good sense and reasoning. Was it worth it? You were supposed to sacrifice, but what if you lost? He thought of how it felt to be moving in the shell down the pond, and his head cleared. Only another rower would understand. He would talk to his brother, but he wished Power and Whelan would disappear, so he did. He glanced at the kitchen window. His mother had moved away from it, and he could see Jack Nugent and Martin Boland coming through the yard—miracle of miracles! Din moved swiftly to the door.

"Come on in, come in. I was just going over to Fox's for a drink of hop beer. I needs one for sure."

Watt jumped to his feet. "You're leaving us without an answer?"

Din grabbed his coat from the hook near the stove. "Goodbye, Watt, John. I'll tell Dan ye was here and ask him if he'll agree to try for a berth with someone else. I knows I done wrong. I'll try to fix it. Mother, will you get John and Watt a dipper of the brew I got in the back room?" He brushed past Watt and John. Martin and Jack smiled nervously and nodded at Watt and John before they set off to catch up to Din. "I'll explain the whole works on the way over to the Rocky Hills," came Din's voice from the yard.

"You're home early, John. Thought you'd be gone all day.

Must be going again soon, are you?" Kate was in the kitchen, bundling herself up against the weather, fixing her heavy shawl. "I'm taking Tommy over to Mother's. We won't be gone too long."

John hadn't said a word since he walked into the house. It was hard to keep a calm face, but he didn't want to show Kate the upset inside him.

Kate pulled the wool cap down over Tommy's ears, licked a finger, and drew it over a smudge by his mouth. "John, it's Christmas. You should be coming with us, my son. Give up that old rowing foolishness. Sure, there'll be enough time to talk about that before August. Ah, John, why don't you give it up entirely?" She stood in front of him, her face sorrowful. "You can't tell me you'd miss the sore hands and sore arse?"

"Don't be at me, Kate. I'm off to Mickey O'Brien's now. There's a whole crowd going there, and I'll be clear of any rowing yarns. John Savage and the Kellys will be there, so it will be cattle talk."

"Oh, and if Bill Pine is up there, there won't be any rowing talk at all, will there? He might have a few things to say about rowing or not rowing with Outer Cove."

John took her hands. She had put on her thickest mitts. "How did you know about Bill Pine?"

"Oh, I have my ways of finding things out. For instance, what was said at the meeting at the liver house." She laughed. "Have yourself a good time at O'Brien's. Come on, Tommy, get a move on."

Chapter 11

"John, John!" He felt Kate's elbow in his side. "Listen!"

He'd been dreaming of the pond, an oar dipping under the surface of the water, the grip of his hands on the wood. But Kate wouldn't let him return there.

"Someone's knocking. Who could it be at this hour?"

John shifted onto his side. He opened his eyes and blindly reached for the box of matches. He lit the lamp, got out of bed, hauled on his pants, and then climbed down the narrow stairway leading to the kitchen. The floor under his feet felt as cold as the ocean. The knocking came again, louder now as John reached the porch. As he put his hand on the latch, it was lifted from the other side, and a man and a thick drift of snow blew in.

"Dear God, is that you, Peter? Peter Cahill? Step in out of that wind."

"I'm sorry to show up at such a shocking hour of the night, John," said Peter's trembling voice, "but young Mary, she got terrible pains in her stomach and they're getting worse. My old horse will never get through this storm. We got to get her to town, to the General. I need a lend of Prince."

"I'm not sure if Prince will behave himself for anyone but me or Kate. I'll take your girl to the hospital, but you or her mother will have to come in the sleigh with me. If this storm don't get any worse, we can likely get to town in an hour and a half."

"John, you're a good man." Peter had stopped shivering, partly because of the warmth of the house, partly because of his relief in hearing John's words. "I'll head back to the house right away and get Mary and Bride ready. The wind is northeast. With any luck, the snow will stop soon." He stepped out into the night and vanished in the blast of the storm.

"I'll be at your house in about twenty minutes, Peter," John yelled at the snowy wall of darkness. He raced back up the stairs to tell Kate about young Mary, then dressed and fled the house.

The wind howled around him as he fought his way from the house to the barn. The kerosene lamp dulled to a flicker, struggling to stay lit. He fought to open the barn door against the gusts pushing him backwards. When he entered the stable, Prince quickly rose up from the straw, turned his head toward John, and nickered. Giant snowflakes smacked against the window in front of Prince's manger and slid down to frame the bottom of the sill, and the roof vent made a whistling sound that swept through the barn. John took the harness from the hooks along the wall. The rattle of the harness stirred Prince, and he began to shuffle his hooves.

"Now, Prince, we got to head out into some weather. We got an important job to do. Go easy now, fella. Go easy." John patted Prince gently on the neck.

The wind pounded the cove and every single thing in it. Snow was blowing around the yard as John and Prince headed out through the gate. The horse took on the night and the squall as if he had taken on such things a hundred times before. John didn't have to slap the reins or raise his voice over the howling gale to get the sleigh moving through the deepening snow. Prince's urgency to get to the Cahills' house seemed greater than John's. The wind, though unabated, had changed slightly in direction, howling just as hard from the north. The gusts whipped up drifts that came almost to the horse's girth. But at least the gale was at their backs.

"She's asleep," Peter said. "The pain was too much for her. She's tired right out. Bride will go with you. They're bundled up warm. At least the wind won't be in your face on the way out. God bless you, John."

John entered the Cahill house and came out carrying Mary. Bride was at his side, holding her skirts tight to her sides. She made her way to the sleigh and climbed into the back of it, holding out her arms for her daughter. "Oh, John, John, my poor Mary," Bride sobbed. "Heaven help us. Will we make it through this blizzard?"

John could barely hear her words through the gale as he got up on the seat. Again, Prince seemed to sense his urgency. The horse plowed through the drifts relentlessly as they passed the wide-open fields of the Kelly and Pine farms. The tailwind seemed to quicken their pace. They encountered no other living soul on the long cold road to town.

Down across the Ross farm they rode, and around the top of the pond. John quickly realized that the lane by the boathouse would likely be blocked with drifts. It would not do to try and climb that steep path. Then he remembered the narrow passage between the west prison wall and the cemetery. He snapped the reins for the first time during the long, difficult ride and headed for the opening to the graveyard.

"Hey, Prince. Hey, boy. Gee up!"

Still showing no signs of fatigue, the horse quickened his stride. The commotion caused Mary to stir. Mumbled words crept out from beneath the pile of blankets.

"Thank God, we're almost there," said Bride. "Don't worry, Mary, my love. We'll soon see the doctor."

John drove the sleigh up to the front of the hospital. He jumped down and helped Bride out, took Mary in his arms, and approached the door. The night porter came to his knock and helped the woman and the girl inside.

Leading Prince behind the hospital, John found a barn and walked him into it, startling the few horses that were there. He put Prince in an empty stall and found some hay for him. Water would come later, when the horse had cooled down. He twisted up a wisp of straw and curried the horse dry. Someone had thrown a moth-eaten blanket on top of the oat bin. John took it off and placed it over his horse.

He walked back to the hospital through the deep snow and knocked on the door. The porter let him in, saying, "I sent a man to go fetch the doctor. That young one is not too good, is she?"

The oak clock on the wall read twenty minutes past three. The warmth from the cast-iron heater radiated through his damp clothes, causing John to drift into a semiconscious state, neither fully asleep nor fully awake. His thoughts raced with images of the blinding snow, of Prince in the hospital barn. Then nothing. The clocked ticked. His head fell forward.

"Sir, sir." John woke quickly, sitting up straight. "Sorry, miss. I fell asleep. How's the girl, how's Mary?"

"Dr. Rendell would like a word with you," said the nurse, a thick-featured woman with fair hair pulled up in a bun and rolls of fat that made her dress look shapeless.

The man beside her was of medium height "Hello. You must have had quite a trip from Outer Cove in this weather. I'm Dr. Rendell." He reached out to shake John's hand. The fisherman's rough hands clasped the soft, firmly fleshed hands of the surgeon. "The whole city is shut down. You are Mary's father?"

"No, sir. I'm a neighbour, sir. John Whelan. How is the girl? How's Mary?"

"She has appendicitis. She'll have to have her appendix removed. I've given her something for the pain, so she's easier now." Dr. Rendell placed a hand on John's shoulder. "You say you are John Whelan. John Whelan the rower?"

"I've rowed in the races, yes."

"You're the stroke with those Outer Cove crews that have won all the titles?"

John shifted in his seat. "Yes, sir. Good crews, we had."

"You're an extraordinary rower, Mr. Whelan. Everyone who follows the regatta knows your name and your record." The doctor's comments surprised John. They made him feel humble, somehow. "I'm keen to know what makes some rowers so refined, while others struggle to grasp the basics. I spend a lot of time on the water, sailing. I've never gotten the hang of rowing, I'm afraid." Rendell laughed. "May I ask you a few questions about your expertise?"

John had never engaged in this type of conversation with a common man, much less a highly educated person, and he was still adrift in the whirl of the night's events. The encounter with Rendell seemed dreamlike and strange. The doctor was almost certainly Bob Sexton's Dr. Herbert Rendell, but he was afraid to ask.

The nurse returned with a tray holding a pot of tea and

a plate with bread and butter on it. The two men sat down together at a small table. John felt himself coming around as he drank and ate. The tea was hot and strong, the bread light, the butter salty and sweet. He sat quietly, occupying himself with the food and drink.

"Mr. Whelan, you're of average build, about my size. Do you find it difficult sometimes to move the boat through the water? I mean, it all depends on force, and there are five others in the boat, too."

"Yes, indeed, it is hard sometimes. But it's like I'm part of the boat. I works hard and the boat gives back." John shrugged his shoulders. "The men behind me are dogs and I'm the tail wagging them." He chuckled. "Great crewmates, I've had. All of them." He looked at the windows on the other side of the room. The heat from the large radiators were keeping them free from the driving snow. The wind had shifted to the northwest and gained strength. The branches of tall maples snapped against the windows.

"Dr. Rendell, sir." John's curiosity got the better of him. "I believes you're the gentleman who gave Bob Sexton the plans for his new boat. My good friend Watt Power and I paid him a visit recently. It's a fine craft he's working on." John looked at the doctor, at his smooth, clean hands. "I beg your pardon, sir, but how do you know so much about boats?"

"Boats are my hobby. I'm a yachtsman, and I have an interest in the architecture of ships. Sexton is a wonderful workman. This boat may prove to be the best one ever rowed on Quidi Vidi." He looked at the tired fisherman, at his big weathered hands which knew so much about the way of a small boat on the water. "So, Mr. Whelan, are you going to row in the new boat Sexton is making? It will be ready for this year's regatta. Only the finishing left to do. He's a gifted builder, very conscientious. This new boat will be very fast."

"I plans on rowing with a crew from the cove. But we're not sure yet if all hands can make the bargain. There are some problems, sir, and . . ." John's voice trailed off. He felt embarrassed for himself, talking about things that would be of no interest to this man.

"What problems are those, Mr. Whelan?"

"Two of the crew might row with Baine Johnston instead of us. They're brothers, and Johnston made them an offer of a berth for the seal hunt. Baine Johnston wants them in their crew on Regatta Day. The catch is, to get the berths they got to promise not to row with anyone else. If the boys make a deal with them, we won't have our crew." John looked away, mumbling. "I'd like to win one more title on the pond, sir, for myself and for the cove. I wants to go back to the rowing because it's what I does best." John pointed at the window that faced the pond, frozen in the darkness of winter. "I loves the races. When I rows, I never feels pain, certainly not the way other men talks about it. Maybe because I'm thinking so hard on the stroke rate it keeps the hurt at bay." His hand moved rhythmically. "Even if I'm not so strong anymore, I wants to lead those men. If I can do that, we won't lose."

"I'm sure the crew trusts that you are still the same John Whelan who has claimed so many victories from the lake." The doctor crossed his legs and smiled at John. "I have no doubt you can meet their expectations." He stood up, walked to the window, rubbed the condensation away, and looked out.

"I must get back to Mary. The child needs an operation right away." He tugged at the stethoscope around his neck. "Looks like the storm is just about over. It will be daylight in a few hours. You might as well stay here until morning. We'll find a bed for her mother." He looked at the man who had braved a fierce storm to save a young girl's life. "And, Mr. Whelan, I'll tell Mrs. Cahill that there won't be a fee."

John rose and reached to shake Dr. Rendell's hand. "Thank you, sir. I'll just go out back and check on my horse."

On the way to the shed, John reflected on the night's business. Sometimes, strange things happened in the middle of a storm.

Chapter 12

"Which one of you is going to Torbay today? One of you has to." Ellen McCarthy polished the teapot to within an inch of its life.

Her two sons looked at each other. "Why?" Dan asked, tying his bootlace. Din looked out the kitchen window. The sun was casting such a brilliant reflection off the snow he had to turn away. That was a good thing, then. "'If Candlemas Day be clear and fine, the rest of winter is left behind; if Candlemas Day be rough and grum, there's more of winter left to come.'"

"Well, it's clear and fine then, so one of ye has got to go to Torbay and bring home a piece of candle Father Clarke has blessed. I knows it's cold, but you can dress up warm."

"Oh, Mother." Dan rolled his eyes. "Do you really think them old candles do any good?"

"If ye two are going after the seals, I needs to have a bit of one of those candles on hand before you leaves, so I can put a few drops of wax on your boots and caps and the rest of it."

"All right, Mother, all right. No need to shout. I'm not deaf like a haddock, and I'm in the kitchen, too."

"What time is the blessing of the candles?" asked Din.

"Four o'clock, same as every year."

"What if the weather turns bad?" Din knew there was no chance of this, but still.

"For heaven's sake, b'ys. Do ye think ye might get lost going over there?" Ellen shook her head. "You never happens to get lost coming back from a dance in Torbay in the pitch black of night." She lifted the damper off the stove and jabbed at the cinders. "One of ye go out to the linny and bring back an armful of wood. Two armfuls. It's going to be a cold night, and I got to get another batch of dough in the oven. There'll be fresh bread to take with you down to the Cobbler when you goes cutting wood." She looked out the window toward the Rocky Hills. "Your poor father." At last, she lowered her voice. "I can see him now, heading off with the horse hitched up to the wood slide. The cold winters, he did not mind. A flask of warm tea, a bit of salt fish, and some hardtack would do him almost a full day."

"We miss Father, too," said Dan as he hauled on his coat. "Now, Mother, don't you worry about wood or candles or anything else. We're not going to run away and leave you alone."

"Except when ye goes to the seal hunt." She looked at her sons.

"Mother, we're not on with Baine Johnston yet." Dan sat down next to her. "We needs to go to the seal hunt. If the salmon or cod prices aren't that good this summer, we're going to have a rough go of it."

"That's right," Din said, back from the linny. He put a pile of junks in the woodbox. "Dan and I are going to see Baine Johnston at the end of the month and tell them we'll sign on with them before they change their minds." He closed the lid of the woodbox with a slam. "We got to sign on soon, because every time I see Watt Power or John Whelan on the road, it's the same question. 'Have you and Dan signed on with them yet?'" Din hunched his back, mimicking Watt, and strutted across the kitchen. "Sometimes I wonder what would be worse—risk being frozen to death on the ice or not go at all and starve to death in the spring of the year." He took a junk of wood and jammed it in the stove. "I thinks I'm going to move to Torbay soon. Getting tired of beating the trails over there to Mass every Sunday. I'm fed up not having our own church."

"Now, my son, if you moves to Torbay, you'll have to row for them. Watt Power would love to hear that, wouldn't he?" Ellen let out a belly laugh and hugged Din.

"Rowing, rowing. Why is it that you can't step two paces in this cove without them saying something about the rowing? I wish someone would pay me to row. At least I'd make a few dollars at it."

"I hear there's riverboats in London that takes passengers. You want to move there, Din, b'y? Me and you in a small boat, we could move a few fares with a two-man crew."

"You're codding me. McCarthy's boat for hire. Gets you to your destination in record time!" There was a roar of laughter from his brother. "Dan, let's not wait until Monday to go to town. Let's go tomorrow. I got to get some new rope at Neal's for the killicks. Fifty fathoms at least, and then we can go straight to Baine Johnston. I knows Mr. Marshall gave us until the end of February to sign on, but we might as well get it over with now. Suppose Watt Power will go off his head if we don't row with the cove," said Din. He and his brother sat at the table, gobbling down as much porridge, salt fish, and bread as they could contain.

"Think about this when you're out rolling on the sea in

March." Ellen stood over them, waving the teapot. "Want more?"

"No, Mother. Got to get going." Dan jumped up from the table and went to get his boots.

"Goddamn silver thaw. I hates it," said Din as he and Dan hitched up the horse to the sleigh. The ground was as slippery as a beach full of caplin and the trees were covered in ice.

"The fog is creeping in over the hills. It's going to turn mild and this will melt. Thank God." Dan picked up Belle's feet and checked her hooves. Her winter shoes with their studs were still in good condition.

"I suppose Neal's aren't going to cause a racket when I goes there and asks for credit for that rope, will they?" Din asked.

"They might, but we don't owe them nothing from last year."

"But suppose they're owed too much by other people?"

Dan shook his head. "Credit . . . what a crooked way to make a dollar."

"I can't wait to go to the hunt," said Din. "Hopes we hit a big patch right away."

"Let's go, Belle." Dan slapped the reins. The mare's shoes gripped the icy path and the sleigh jolted toward town.

It was well before noon when they turned onto Duckworth Street. Horses and men slipped along the icy streets, the manure making them even more treacherous. The port city in winter was cold and dirty. Dan waited outside Neal's for Din, watching the spectacle that was St. John's.

"Good news, Dan, good news," said Din as he jumped in the sleigh. "Mr. Neal said there won't be a problem getting the rope when the salmon fishery opens. He took my order. I told him we had berths for the hunt, and he took that as a sign that we'd be good to pay up. We'd better head up and see Mr. Marshall."

Dan spat his wad of tobacco into a snowbank already sullied with coal dust, horse piss, and manure. "By the looks of the crowd around town, I think we made the right move coming out today instead of waiting until Monday. Never seen the like of it. We'd best tie up the mare at Haymarket Square and walk up to Ayres Cove."

The commotion outside Baine Johnston's office was being made by an assembly of rough-looking men. The atmosphere was near fever pitch as more men lined up to meet with the company representative. The younger they were, the dirtier they looked; they used dirt to disguise their age, and it often worked. Men, especially young men, were desperate for money. They had weighed the dangers of the hunt against the risk of being broke for months ahead and had decided to throw in their lot with the hunt.

"Please don't come into the office in groups larger than two," said the clerk. "Give Mr. Marshall your last name and tell him where you are from. Now, stop the pushing and shoving. I will let you in the office two at a time. Do you hear me?" The clerk, a short, stout man with uneasy eyes, held them back. He plucked up his courage, which took fuel from his anxiety. "What a rancid smell. When was the last time you men washed?"

Dan and Din had been through this before. Each year the same mayhem ensued. They waited in line and entered the warm office together. Photographs and paintings of sealing ships hung precisely on the walls. A fine pair of leather boots had been placed to dry next to the stove. A thin man sat behind the desk smoking a cigarette. The brothers gave their names.

"You're not signing on with this company," said Marshall, as he picked up the pen and tipped back the chair.

"What? Sure, you told us before Christmas we were certain to get berths on your ship." Din had turned blood red and was advancing toward the desk. Hearing his raised voice, the clerk turned away from the door and looked at Din. Perhaps they would have to send one of the boys for a constable. It had been necessary before.

"All I can tell you is that you're not going to the hunt on the *Southern Cross*. Now, you had better go see Mr. Halley at Bowring's right away. I'm busy. I've got to see the rest of those men."

"Mr. Marshall," said Dan, shocked and confused. "You got to tell us what's going on. What's this about Bowring's?"

"You'd better move along." The clerk motioned them out, and they went. Two more men slipped in as Dan and Din left. The clerk grimaced at them as soon as their backs were through the door. Dirty baymen.

The brothers half walked and half ran up Water Street to Steers's Cove, stumbling and bumping into other people who were trying to keep their footing on the slippery sidewalks. When they reached Bowring's office, they pushed past the waiting men.

"Where the hell do you think you're going?" a haggard-faced fellow yelled. "I've been waiting here all morning. Get back in the goddamn line." The crowd started murmuring, which soon turned into a sound like the rumble of a large, angry cat. A passing constable slowed and then stopped. He stared at the men through narrowed eyes, tapping his stick against his leg. The noise died down.

Din and Dan brushed by the clerk, who grabbed

ineffectually at their coats, muttering furiously. They slowed down and entered Halley's office.

The man behind the desk raised his head from the papers spread over it. "You look like twins. The McCarthy brothers?"

"Yes, sir. I'm Din, and this is my brother, Dan. We were told to come here."

"That's right. You have berths aboard the *Aurora*. That's an order from Mr. Bowring, Mr. Edgar Bowring." Din and Dan looked at each other in amazement. "You board her on March 7. Captain Kean is expecting you. Now sign here." He passed them the register.

Chapter 13

The tiny wooden beads slipped through Ellen's small hands. It was Saturday night and she had just completed the Joyful Mysteries. Din and Dan didn't spend much time at home in the evenings like they used to. And now the seal hunt was looming—both of them gone at the same time, on the same ship. She stopped rocking and held the beads to her breast. She often woke at night wondering if the boys were safe at home. Sometimes they were and sometimes they weren't, but they always came home eventually. Her body trembled. She began to rock again, trying to stem the gloomy thoughts. She began to pray again, fighting the loneliness. Every once in a while she got up to stoke the fire. The sound of the burning wood was her greatest comfort during the long, cold winter nights. She wished for June and the summer fishery, the long days and short nights. Her sons would leave for the traps before dawn and be back for breakfast. Now they were going off to the icefields in the dead of winter. Long days on the pans for them, longer nights in the cove for her. It was only two years ago that all those men from the *Greenland* died, frozen to death in the night after they got separated from their ship. And not ten years since the Trinity Bay disaster. One hundred or more landsmen hunting seals in the bay when a blizzard came up;

there had been a score or more of widows and orphans out of that one. She went to the woodbox and took out the dry spruce to feed her fire.

"When the bishop blesses the fleet, make sure you are both blessing yourself, too. You'll need every blessing and lots of good luck out there on the ice." Ellen tried to keep her hands steady as she helped her sons pack their boxes of supplies, filling them with extra woollen mitts, socks, and whatever else would help keep them warm and dry. She looked out the kitchen window at one point. There was a young, black-haired woman heading toward the house. "Dan, there's Liz coming up the lane." She turned to him and squeezed his arm. "I hopes you comes back in one piece. She's a fine young woman, and the two of ye are a grand match."

"Mother, I knows a thing or two about a thing or two," said Dan. "Liz and I are pretty content. You don't mind her staying around until we leaves to go out to the ship? You don't mind that, do you?"

"Not at all, my son, not at all."

"We better get going soon, Mother," said Din. "We can let Liz off in Logy Bay and then us three can go on to town."

"Not likely, Din. Sure, what are you thinking? Liz is coming to town with us, and then she'll drive back with Mother. Mother would like a bit of company—you knows the way women are. They likes to have a gab." He laughed and lunged away from Ellen, who had picked up the broom and was shaking it at him.

"All right, b'y. No need to start a racket. Our mare can haul a half a dozen people in that sleigh," said Din. "Sara is going to meet us at the docks. One less body to bring to town." He rolled his eyes, slapped Dan on the side of the head, and grinned.

The winter snow, solidly packed along Logy Bay Road,

made an easy haul for Belle. She sped along, the bells on the sleigh tinkling cleanly in the clear air. Smoke rose straight up from the chimneys of the sparsely spaced houses.

There was barely room for Belle and the slide beside the pier where the *Aurora* was docked. "Where's that Sara to?" Din paced, never taking his eyes off the crowd at the docks. Hundreds of men with their boxes of supplies milled about.

"This place is busier than the regatta," Dan said.

Many sealers had come from far-flung bays to be part of the annual ritual. Their journeys would be the stuff of stories told at night in the holds of the steamers after a day of killing seals. The youngest men from the outharbours, in their late teens, seemed both excited and fearful—no girlfriends or mothers in St. John's to wish them a safe voyage and good luck at the hunt.

"There she is." Din stood up in the slide and waved frantically at a slight, fair-haired girl in a woollen cape and cap. "Over here!" he shouted.

"Where were you, Din? I thought you'd never show up." Sara pouted at Din.

"Oh, don't fuss me, love. Poor Belle had to haul the four of us out over the road. Not that easy, even for a young mare." Din leaned ahead and patted Belle's flank.

Sara sniffed the cold air loudly and then ran to Din as he got down from the sleigh. They both lost their balance on the ice. "Mother of God, Din, be careful out there, will you? I thinks about the danger all the time." She covered his lips and face with kisses.

Scores of men lined the docks waiting for Bishop Howley to arrive and bestow the church's blessing upon the sealers for a safe return.

"Now, Sara. I'll be back before you know it, and we'll be ordering windows for our house." Din took her arms and held her a few inches away from him so he could get a breath. But it wasn't long before she had her arms around his neck again. Passersby laughed, and Din felt the heat come into his face. He wriggled away and looked at the harbour.

But she was relentless. "I prays you'll do well on the *Aurora*, Din. But mostly I prays you'll come home alive and in one piece." She pulled him to her again. Her body was warm, and he could almost taste the lavender water she had put behind her ears. His legs suddenly felt limp.

Ellen looked at Dan and Liz, who were in each other's arms in the rear seat of the sleigh. "Now, you two. In public! I never saw the like. Time to get going."

"How many days do you think you'll be gone?" Liz asked.

"Twenty. Maybe less if we strike a big patch right away."

"Twenty days," she moaned.

"I got to go aboard, Liz." He kissed her again. "I wished I could just take you in my mouth like a dog and carry you with me."

Liz shivered. "Dan, Dan, watch out for yourself. Mind you don't do nothing foolish."

Northerly gales pounded the cove for the second day. The windows of every home had been masked with snow by the blast of the late winter blizzard. The McCarthys were among a dozen men from Outer Cove who had gone to the hunt. The other men in the rowing crew visited Ellen often. Martin Boland and Jack Nugent often came together, checking on the animals in the barn, bringing Ellen water from the well, and filling the woodbox. For the last two nights, however, she had been a prisoner in her own house. She had slept badly, waking often and praying for the safe return of her sons.

They had been gone for nearly two weeks. If they had hit the seals and done well, that would add to the weight of the ship. The captains of the vessels were under orders to take as many pelts as they could load, but a fully-loaded ship in heavy seas was a disaster in the making. She hoped their skipper knew the limits of his boat in all weathers.

Watt made his way down O'Rourke's Lane through the snowdrifts until he decided it was easier to go through the open meadow, where the snow had mostly blown away. He struggled up to Ellen's door, pushing the snow away from it with his boot. She was sitting in the kitchen, a cup of tea between her hands.

"Dear Lord, Watt. I'm nearly out of my mind stuck in the house alone. Do you think they survived this storm? I haven't slept one solid hour for the past two nights."

Ellen's blue eyes were red with fatigue. She seemed to have aged since Watt last saw her. He felt a sudden surge of pity. Women had it hard, so they did.

"If they're in the ice pack and they don't get rammed with the raftering ice, they should be fine," said Watt. "You got to hope that they weren't in open water with that gale. Safer to be stuck in the ice than fighting the swell. Bowring's got a good skipper with Kean. If anyone can make it through heavy seas, he can."

"I can't take this not knowing nothing. There must be some news getting into town. Can you give me a hand to hitch up Belle to the sleigh? I got to get into town today and try to get some word on the fleet."

"Mrs. McCarthy, even though the storm's over, it will be

a rough go to get to town in this mess. Do you want me to go with you?"

"Liz will go with me. I'm miserable company right now, but she won't mind."

The waters outside the Narrows gleamed white with pack ice, and a brisk east wind kept any warmth from the blinding sun at bay. The month of March was more generous with light than February, but the cold air offered little comfort. As the mare and sleigh clipped past the Prince's Rink in the east end of St. John's, Ellen snapped the reins to encourage the mare to trot more quickly. The streets became busier and busier, with pedestrians and box carts, horses, sleighs, and more horses. Shopkeepers and passersby were standing on the sidewalks talking, their faces looking drawn. There seemed to be tension in the air. Ellen shivered involuntarily. She waved to Mr. Burke, who was standing in front of his shop, but he didn't seem to notice her.

A chorus of paperboys stood at a street corner. "Sealing ship missing!" cried the biggest of the four ragged lads on the corner, waving a copy of one of the morning papers.

Ellen felt as if she had been hit in the face. She passed the reins to Liz, who had barely said a word during their entire journey. The girl whimpered as Ellen got down from the sleigh.

"Boy, boy," Ellen called. "Which ship? Which ship?"

"Don't know, missus. I can't read. The paper is one cent to buy." He began to walk away.

"Come here, come back here." The boy turned around obediently. Ellen reached for the copy he was holding out toward her. Before it reached her hands, she saw the large, bold print: **No Sight of Southern Cross**. Panic choked her as she snatched the paper and scanned the small print below the headline. The Baine Johnston ship had not been seen for some time, according to the ships that had returned. She quickly looked for the *Aurora* in the list of returning ships. There it was. Relief came quickly, her rapid heartbeat the only reminder that for a few minutes she had been sure her world had come to an end. She gave the boy his penny, and suddenly found herself putting her arms around him. He stank, but she didn't care. He was her angel of deliverance.

Chapter 14

"I never thought I'd be so happy to see the rain and fog again." Dan ran the file through the teeth of the bucksaw. "Day after day, swinging a gaff until me arm nearly fell off. Almost blind from the sun on the ice." He squinted hard and shuddered.

"We'll be complaining soon enough if we don't get good weather," replied Din as he hung the saw on the wooden dowel. They stepped out of the barn. Din looked down at the river. "Soon be time to set the salmon nets."

"Yes, and start rowing," said Dan. "It's a good way to get back at the fishing. At least you're not hauling up a ton of fish every day, like the cod. I likes the look of salmon. They're strong." He rolled up the sleeve of his jacket to show his massive forearm. "Strong like me," he laughed, and gently shoved his brother out of the way.

"I hear the *Southern Cross* made it back to port safely. Shag all pelts in her hold. The b'ys only got twenty-two dollars each." Din shook his head. "Stuck in pack ice off Baccalieu Island for ten days."

Dan picked up a large log and placed it on the sawhorse. "What are you going to buy with the money from the hunt?"

"Let's hope there's some left after the bills are all squared."

"And if there is?"

"Don't know. You?"

"I already spent most of mine." Dan reached under his jumper and brought out a jeweller's box, then quickly stowed it away again.

Din laughed. "Might as well tell me what it is, before I tells you. A ring, I suspects." Din grabbed Dan by the shoulders. "So, are we going to have a bit of a time someday soon?" He swung Dan around the yard and they both fell on the wet ground. "You're getting married—I knows you are." Din got to his feet and stamped the ground. "Liz is a grand girl, Dan. I'd have her meself, but I'm taken already, and you're the next best fella to me around here." He laughed again.

"I never said I was getting married." Dan had a huge grin on his face. He couldn't hold his happiness inside any longer. "Don't you go telling anyone yet. I got to go to Liz's this evening. Tell her, I mean ask her. Talk to her father. Then I'll come home and tell Mother."

"When are we going to celebrate? You got to have a time."

"Friday night. Now you be quiet for the rest of the day, you hear?"

The celebration at the Mccarthy house began before darkness fell, and people came and went all throughout the night. There was a constant babble of voices.

"When are ye two getting hitched?" asked a man from Middle Cove.

"Are ye going to build a house next to your mother's? Live in Logy Bay?" said someone.

"I don't know," said Liz, throwing up her hands and laughing. She had been blushing and laughing all evening. "I only knows one thing. We won't be getting married until that cursed race is over in August."

"Mother, don't put any more wood in that stove or we'll die with the heat," Din yelled across the room.

Someone had brought a fiddle, another an accordion. The dancing was going full tilt and the spruce beer was flowing. Black rum was making its way around the kitchen.

"I'll have a swig of that." Mike Kinsella reached out and grabbed the bottle. He swallowed a mouthful, then coughed like death was near certain, before passing it on to the next fellow. "Do they think of me in Ireland?" he shouted, collapsing on the daybed.

"If you're either bit hungry, there's a nice pot of rabbit stew on the stove. Grab a plate and dig in," Ellen said to the crowd, shouting to be heard above the melee. "Lots of bread on the table, too, thanks to Kate Whelan. And pies and cakes—you needn't be shy!" She was mostly ignored as the dancers and the talkers competed for space in the stifling kitchen. "Don't break the floorboards with those big boots there, Boland." Martin Boland danced a jig, urged on by the clapping hands of a house full of revellers.

"I'm some glad the crew showed up, Dan," said Din into his brother's ear. "They're not holding it against us, then." He swayed a bit, clutched Dan's arm, belched, and tried to unscramble his slurred speech. "All that racket about whether the crew would stay together. Lucky you was in Logy Bay when Watt and John showed up here St. Stephen's Day. I never thought I'd ever speak to the two of them again." The brothers clinked their glasses and emptied them in one swallow.

Dan spotted Watt sitting on the woodbox and squeezed his way through the crowd to him. Watt leaned close to Dan and spoke. Suddenly, they both stood up. Dan beckoned to Liz. When she joined them, the three huddled together. Watt and Dan nodded and smiled at each other and held a handshake longer than Liz could bear to look.

Dan took his hand from Watt's and turned to face the crowd. After he'd let out a roar that made the room go quiet, he said, "Liz and me wants to thank all of ye for coming here tonight. And we'll see ye all again at the wedding!" The kitchen erupted with applause and hearty calls. "Now, before we get back to the dancing, Watt Power has a few words to say."

Watt hauled himself up with the help of the warming closet on the stove. The kitchen grew still as he walked over and placed himself in front of the picture of Christ on the wall.

"I don't want to take anything away from the occasion tonight," he said, nodding at Dan and Liz. "I wishes the happy couple the very best, as do we all. But I wants to say one thing now, and Liz won't mind, will you, girl?" Liz shook her head, smiling at Watt. He shifted his eyes around the room, stopping briefly to look at each of the faces of the other six men in the crew. "This crew, with this man on stroke oar," he said, pointing to John and slurring a little as he tugged at his greying beard, "will bust my record time in the *Myrtle*. We'll do it for all of ye here tonight, for the whole cove."

"You're the fella to lead them, Mr. Power," Ellen called out. There were cheers, and then the party resumed, roaring on into the early morning.

The break of dawn had passed hours before anyone in the McCarthy home stirred. Fog wrapped around the house like kelp clinging to the rocky shoreline.

"Oh, my head," Din cried out. "I got to get some pain medicine into the house before the wedding." He buried his head in the daybed's feather pillow.

"You got to know when to quit. I seen ye with the jug full to the brim more than once last night." Ellen was sweeping away the evidence of the many feet that had danced into the daylight hours. "Dan, aren't you and Din going to the salmon berth draw tonight?"

"That's not tonight, is it, Mother?"

"Yes, it is. You'd better get up and have something to eat. Get yourself straightened out."

The chill winds of March had been replaced by the milder southerly breezes of April. Din Croke slowly inched his way along the fence where he had hung his gillnet, checking it for holes and tears. He had just begun his inspection of the full sixty fathoms which stretched from his house to the woods near the Big River, measuring each opening in the mesh to make sure it was identical in size to the others. When necessary, he would guide a needle threaded with manila twine through the net, securing each new piece with a knot tight enough to withstand the strength of a shark. Not that he ever wanted to see such a powerful fish, much less catch one.

"Hello there, Croke," said a voice behind him. He fastened another knot and turned. Watt Power was leaning against the side of the barn.

"Watt, you're a bit off course today. Thought you'd be over at Middle Cove beach getting your salmon nets ready."

"I'm all finished. Me nets were in pretty good shape." Watt struck a match, lit his pipe, and walked to where Din was standing. "A small amount of mending. Two more weeks and we'll be back on the water."

"You must have something on your mind, do you, b'y?

What brings you here? You never came to talk about cattle."

"You're pretty clever, Croke," Watt said, laughing. "I was strolling back from the beach and I got to thinking. I had this idea—what with your salmon berth being right next to Martin Boland and Jack Nugent's, and you being a lone hand at the nets." He raised his eyebrows and took a deep draw from his pipe.

He walked up to the net-covered fence and touched the twine, passing his fist though the openings. "You're a big man. I needs a strong fella like you in the middle of the boat, right behind Din McCarthy. That way, I'll have the biggest men where it counts, in the middle of the shell where the crew's weight is felt the most. You'll be number three oar.

"I needs you to get used to following someone in a boat. Not Whelan, just some experienced hands. So here's my plan." He twirled his long whiskers. "How do you feel about sharing a boat with Nugent or Boland when you goes out after the salmon?" Watt drew closer to Croke, trying to gauge his reaction. "Here's how I sees it. They shares the same boat and you have your own. So one day you rows out to the nets with Nugent, the next day with Boland. Whichever one you're not rowing with can take your boat. You'll row every day, get used to following a good man and used to the timing of the blades." Watt held his hands in front of him and moved them rhythmically up and down like slicing swords. "When the salmon is over, we'll start practising on Quidi Vidi."

Croke smacked his hands together. "I likes your idea. Make no wonder they calls you the wise man. I gets a bit bored out on the water alone sometimes. And it's much easier to haul nets with two men, especially when the sea's rough. But did you ask Martin and Jack about me rowing with them?"

Watt looked away. He walked along the rock boundary wall, pretending to check the fenceposts for firmness. "Don't worry, my son. They're eager to have you in the boat. I knows they never said nothing when your name was brought up at the liver house after Jack Doran said he couldn't row. That's just their way. If it had to come to a vote between you and Pine, they'd have picked you." He placed his hand on Croke's shoulder. "Since you're agreeable to the plan, I'll have them convinced by the end of the day. No trouble at all." He took a puff from his pipe. A small blue trail of smoke drifted away and disappeared.

John and Martin tipped the boat over, revealing the open seams of its smooth var bottom. "You done a fine thing, taking in young Tommy Slater," said Martin. "I don't know what would've become of him but for you two. Orphanage, I suppose."

"Tommy's a fine lad. Smart, too. Remembers everything, he does," said John. "A few days ago I heard him talking to Kate." John stepped back from the boat. "You won't believe what he said. He knows the name of every single salmon berth, all fourteen of them. And who drew each one. Now, how do you suppose he remembers that? And why would he want to?"

"He must be doing good in school, then," said Martin.

"Yes, real good," said John proudly. "Miss Morrissey thinks he's a wonder. He helps her out with the other youngsters when she's busy."

The two men carefully tapped wads of oakum into the seams until they were tight.

"Do you suppose we'll beat Torbay in the races?" asked Martin. "Do you really think we can win?"

John stopped working and put the oakum aside. "I didn't like what Clements said to me at Scanlan's, but that won't change the way I rows. It may change the way he rows, though, or how Torbay rows."

He took out his pocket knife and opened it. "Those cocky bastards made the challenge. Let's see if they can live up to it." He ran the knife blade along the bottom of the boat, cutting the loose strands of fibre hanging from the newly closed seams. Then he ran his hands over the bottom, from bow to stern.

Martin reached down to the pile of rope at his feet. He took an end and started to form circles. Never taking his eyes off John, he placed the rope circles, one on top of the other, over and over, until it became a coil.

"Martin, we knows what to do when Watt gives us the command. Neddy Gosse is going to be equal to the task with the Torbay crew. He's a fine cox." John picked up a jigger and let the line run free from the spool. Holding it in front of Martin, he began to swing it like the pendulum of a clock. "I rows the way I thinks. I rows the same way this jigger swings, except for . . ." His eyes followed the arc of the moving jigger back and forth, back and forth. "The only difference between this jigger swinging and the oar in me hand is the time. The jigger takes a second, but I'm a bit longer than that making a stroke with the oar. Watt told me. I knew the stroke length took longer, but he timed it." He grinned as he walked slowly around the boat. The crunch of beach rocks beneath his boots competed with the noise of the heavy waves hitting the bulkhead at Boy's Cove. The waves exploded on impact, sounding like distant gunfire, and spray rose like smoke.

"You got to feel the oar in your hand when it's out of the water. There's no thinking to be done when the blade is in the water, that's just the work part. You thinks when the blade is in the air. Although there's not much time to think then, is there?" He tossed the jigger to the ground. "When Croke rows with you or Jack tomorrow, remind him every time he puts an oar in his hand about what I just said. He's a big man, he already knows how to pull on the oar."

Another huge wave burst against the rocky cove. The sound vibrated through John like the sound of the starter's gun.

Chapter 15

The child-sized punt lay against the sill of the barn door. Its seat had been torn free and was sitting in the spring grass. There was a small hole in its bottom. John picked it up and carried it into the house.

"Where's Tommy to this morning, Kate?" He laid the broken pieces of the punt against the table.

Kate looked at him. "Dear God in heaven. What happened to his boat?"

John shook his head. "Where is he?"

"He's down at the Big River. I thought he had the boat with him."

John made his way down the steep ravine behind the empty Slater house, pushing aside the alder branches invading the narrow path. He stopped halfway down and listened. There was the sound of water being disturbed. When he got to the bottom of the ravine and stepped out of the alders, he saw Tommy tossing rocks into a dark pool. John cleared his throat and the boy turned around. When he saw John, his small legs made an attempt at scrambling up the slippery bank, but he slid back to the edge of the water.

"My son, don't run away. What are you scared of me for?" Hurt, John went to help him stand up.

"Leave me alone." Tommy moved back until he could go no farther. The deep pool was just a few feet away. Tears streamed down his dirt-covered cheeks. "I don't want to live with you and Aunt Kate no more. I wants to go home."

John crouched down, his back against a large rock. Slowly, he reached out to touch Tommy, but the boy backed closer to the water's edge.

"Go away. Leave me alone." Tommy's words came out on the back of short, choking breaths.

John felt tears come into his own eyes. He picked up a sharp stone at his feet and held it tightly so that it would dig into his palm. "We can fix the boat, Tommy. It's a tough little punt. You know, we needs to be tough sometimes, too, to make things better for ourselves."

Tommy raised his head and looked at John. "I never meant to break it. I got mad." He walked slowly toward John, who moved toward him, until they were face to face. John put out his arms and pulled the child to him. He smiled when he realized Tommy was wiping his nose against his flannel shirt.

"That's all right, b'y. I gets mad sometimes, too."

"Yes, I knows you do. I heard you tell Aunt Kate you was mad at that man Clements from Torbay."

John grinned. "Yes, I was some mad at him. Let's go back to the house and see if we can get Kate to make some fudge. You likes fudge, don't you?"

"What's fudge?"

"It's like candy. Real sweet." John licked his lips. "Especially Kate's fudge. Do you want to ride partway home on my back?" He felt the boy's head nod against his chest. "All right, then." John bent down and Tommy climbed up, wrapping his small arms around John's big shoulders.

Juncos were chirping in the trees as they climbed the steep gorge. A fox sparrow added two notes' worth to their song.

Tommy squeezed John's shoulders. "I'm not mad no more, Uncle John. And I can't wait to get home."

Chapter 16

Jack and Martin hurried along with their grub boxes. Hungry gulls screamed overhead, struggling to gain control of their flight as the gusty winds tossed them up and down. The roaring Big River drove torrents of water down through the valley to the ocean, turning the salty tide at the beach brown.

"I heard Francis Tapper muttering in church yesterday morning. He was sitting in the pew behind me and Mary," said Jack.

"That arse. He can never keep his maw shut. He'll never smother, that's for sure. Always got his trap going. Win or lose, he got something to say." Martin picked up a large stone and smashed it to the ground.

"Jeez, Martin, don't take much to get you riled up this morning. Have a rough night?" He stepped away from Martin as they walked down under the bridge toward the boats.

"No, b'y. I had a good sleep. The thought of that Tapper mouthing off poisons me. Tell me, what did that prate-box say?"

"He said, 'We'll be so far ahead of you on the pond Regatta Day, all you'll see is the back of our heads.' I couldn't believe what I was hearing. In church, too."

"You got to tell Watt," said Martin. "In fact, tell everyone in the cove that Frankie boy is shooting off his gob again." Martin reached his boat. He grabbed the thole-pins and jammed them into the holes in the gunwale. "Where's Croke? He's rowing with me this morning, isn't he?"

"Here he comes." Jack was anxious to steer clear of Martin's angry face.

"Sorry I'm late, b'ys. Jeezly cow got off her rope and went clear of the yard. Found her down by the river. How are ye this morning?" Din Croke wiped the sweat from his brow with his shirtsleeve.

"I'm not feeling so good." Martin threw a coil of rope into the boat, sending the oars flying out over the side.

"I hopes you're not angry with me. Couldn't let the cow roam free all day."

"It's not you, Din. Tell him, Jack. Tell Din about your not-so-holy experience at Mass yesterday."

They shoved off from the landwash against a biting northwest wind. May was the month of Mary, but the weather was nothing like the gentle Mother of God today. Martin jumped in the bow as it cleared the shore. Din already had his oars out, single-handedly moving the boat out to sea before Martin could even begin to row.

"The wind is enough to cut ye," Din grunted. "If we can make it to the Point in less than half an hour, we won't be cold very long." He and Martin settled in with the fine ash oars, clipping over the rising waves, driving the blades into the crest, pushing the punt away from the water.

"Old Watt don't ever seem to stop thinking about the rowing," Din mumbled, as he strained the muscles of his long frame to keep the boat off the shoals at Witty Cove. It wasn't easy keeping in stroke with Martin. The punt bobbed and tipped, the waves almost coming over the bow. His arms began to tire. He pushed his feet against the bottom of the seat in front of him to keep the pressure on the oar. Martin had set a brutal pace.

"Watt's a devil." Martin laughed. "He's hiding up there in the tuckamore, watching. Guaranteed."

Martin could hear Din gasping for breath as they passed Half Way Rock. He didn't ease the pace. Watt had told him to train Croke, and that's what he would do.

Din didn't lessen his efforts, either. He was too strong and too stubborn to surrender to the waves that broke against the sides of the small boat. His oars turned up huge white wakes with each drive of the blades. The punt flew across the water, against the tide. The boat and its contents seemed weightless. Ten minutes more to the nets. He was beginning to feel winded.

"How long will Watt have us practise on the pond when we first start?" Din hollered over the wind. "Fifteen minutes? Twenty?" A wave splashed into the boat, drenching one of his oar handles.

"It won't be too long, rowing without stopping."

"Won't be as rough as this, neither."

"What, are you getting tired?" Din shrugged his broad shoulders and Martin laughed. "We got a whole bunch of drills that Watt takes us through just to get our timing right. It will be at least a week, maybe ten spins, before we get used to those shells." Martin took a deep pull on the fresh salt air. He was feeling the effects of their hard rowing, too. "My job today is to be your rate man, the stroke oar. I'm no John Whelan, but I've rowed behind John before, learned a few things. We can talk in this boat, but when we're on the pond there's no talking, unless you're on the verge of death. At least, there's no talking where you and I will sit."

The boat went by Din's salmon net at Klondike. A few hundred feet before the Point, Martin increased the stroke rate. The jump in pace confused Din. He struggled to keep up. "What are you doing, you bloody arse?" he gasped. "We're almost there; time to slow down."

"No talking, Din." Martin kept his grin to himself.

They rowed the final few strokes to the net, crossed the lead rope anchored to the cliff, stopped rowing, and collapsed on their oars, chests heaving. Martin reached back to shake Din's hand. When he released the sweaty grip, he looked down at his hands. They had blood on them—Din's blood.

Din battled the swell, trying to keep his balance. He reached down into the water to grab the cork floats. The cold salt water stung the open cuts on his hand.

"Ah, damn it," he said, grimacing.

"We'll make quick work hauling this, Din." Martin grabbed the net and started to pull it along the boat. "Let's get at it, don't want to be out here too long and catch a chill." The wind cut across the water, making the boat roll as they struggled to haul the net. They worked the punt toward the tarnished silver reflection of a fish down in the choppy brine. The salmon, still alive and thinking perhaps that it would be free again, fought as they hoisted it into the boat. Martin whistled. "He's some size—must be twenty pounds. Here come two more. All big ones today. " They pulled the fish over the side.

Another shimmering flash deep in the water up ahead, then another. The mighty swimmers were trapped now, some of them drifting lifelessly under the swells, others struggling with the last ounce of strength in their powerful bodies to break clear of the mesh.

"These will bring a good price. Haul away, Din, haul away."

They brought the net to the boat again and again, moving it through the water, checking every fathom. The work seemed easy when the catch was good. When the boat was full, they set the net back out, hoping tomorrow's catch would be just as plentiful. Reaching the end, they tossed the marker buoy back into the sea and grabbed the oars.

"Don't worry about me talking on the way to shore," said Din. "I'm too tired to talk. Got to save my breath for the rowing."

"We'll check your net on the way back," said Martin, laughing. "You'll get a little break." Thirty minutes to shore, he thought. The wind had shifted to the east, a tailwind to help them home. He looked at the sky. A silent prayer answered, perhaps.

Chapter 17

Kate took the pans of bread from the oven and tipped them upside down. The golden-brown loaves fell out on the oilcloth. She flipped them upright and covered their tops with butter. It gave off a sweet aroma as it melted.

"Aunt Kate," asked Tommy. "Can I have the heel? With molasses?"

Kate sliced a thick piece and passed it to him. Steam puffed out of the cut loaf. "Here, Tommy. You knows where the molasses is."

"I helped John plant the seed potatoes yesterday. Here's how I did it." Tommy placed one foot ahead of the other. "My feet are small, so two of my boots are as long as of one of Uncle John's. That's how far apart I put the seed potatoes in the garden."

"You're pretty clever to figure that out. Now eat your bread before it cools off."

"Uncle John's home." Tommy looked out the window, his mouth full of bread.

John felt a sting in his buttocks as he rose from the seat of the cart. He reached down into the back of his pants and felt dampness. The chafed flesh was bleeding. *So it begins*, he thought. There was no getting past the blisters, aches, and pains of trying to win a championship. He shrugged his shoulders and began walking up the lane to the house, whistling, his coat draped over his shoulder, his cap in his hand. He opened the door to the porch. "Fresh bread. Give us a slice or two of that, missus. I'm gut-foundered." John's eyes widened as though he'd never seen the likes of Kate's baking.

Kate got down a plate and cut two slices from the loaf. "Tea's in the pot. Supper is going to be a bit late. How was your first spin on the pond?" She glanced at Tommy and grinned. Tommy smiled. There was molasses stuck to both ends of his mouth.

"I shouldn't say nothing outside the crew, but Croke has a fair bit to learn. He's eager and strong, but he keeps driving the oar down in the water like he's trying to kill something with it." John took a sip of tea, washing the bread down. "The boat rocks a lot. Could be a number of reasons for that." He swayed in the chair as he ate. After he was finished, he got up and went to the window that faced the ocean. Prince was leaning over the fence of the horse pound, looking at the house. "Watt will figure Croke out, make him a rower." He scratched his stubbled chin, turned to Kate, and cracked a smile. "Tommy, you go out and take Prince some water, now. Come on, we goes and gets a bucketful."

Prince began to neigh and toss his head as the porch door opened. His black mane flew in the warm June breeze. His round, dark eyes focused on the emerging figures.

"What's he making that noise for?"

"That's horse talk, young Thomas." John laughed, and handed him the heavy bucket full of water. "You're strong enough to carry this. Be careful you don't spill it."

Tommy staggered out into the yard and went to Prince's enclosure, gripping the pail with both hands. Prince shuffled his hooves as the boy walked toward him. John watched them for a moment, then turned and went back in the house. Kate was sitting by the stove darning a sock. She looked up as he came in.

"So, John, tell me. What if Croke don't work out with the crew? Is there anyone else you can get?"

"I don't know, Kate. I haven't given that a thought. We knew Croke was a risk. He's like an ox, but rough." He gulped the rest of his tea, which had cooled off. Kate's question was something John didn't want to hear voiced. He went to the window, looked out at Tommy watering Prince, and then returned to his chair.

"This bread is some good. Did you do something different to it?"

He rose again, walked to the stove, lifted the damper, and glared into the smouldering ashes. More than anyone else in the boat, perhaps even more than Watt, he did not want to forfeit meeting the Torbay crew at the starting line on Regatta Day. But if the crew failed to form . . . He couldn't imagine it. He'd have to walk to Mass in St. John's for the rest of his life if Torbay won. That would be his penance for losing.

"There's no other men in the cove to pick from. The Roches and Kinsellas are going back at it this year. That's another crew from here. You knows about that crowd. Rowing to keep their berths on the *Terra Nova*. Never much good at it, but we got to race against them, too."

"John, will this be your last year?" She walked up behind him and wrapped her arms around him. "You'll soon be thirty-seven, John," she whispered in his ear. "You can't row forever. You might hurt that strong back of yours. Now that wouldn't be good, would it?" She kissed him on the neck.

John felt the warmth of her hands on his folded arms through the thin material covering them. "I'm pretty sure it's my last year. Pretty damn sure."

The kitchen door opened with a bang. "Prince wants more water." Tommy handed a startled John the empty bucket.

Chapter 18

Ellen tossed a pan of bread crumbs to the hens in the yard and closed the screen door.

"Mother!" Dan thumped through the hallway. "Where's Din?"

"He's not back from the beach yet. What are you bawling out for? I'm just here in the porch." Ellen shook her head. "Aren't you going for a spin on the pond? My son, you better have something to eat, you can't row on an empty stomach."

"No, I got to go now. Tell Din to come by Liz's on the way to the pond." He took a dipper of water from the bucket and drank it down, water spilling from the sides of his mouth onto his shirt. He grabbed his mother and kissed her so hard she squeaked, and then he tore off out of the house. The hens scattered, clearing a path for him as he ran in all directions like a hawk. He slowed his pace only when he was nearly at Liz's house. The evening sun was still high, and the warm blue haze seemed to be squeezing the water out of the air onto his overheated body. He took a handkerchief from his shirt pocket and wiped his face and neck.

"Come in, Dan, come in and sit down. Let me get you some water." Liz got a tumbler full of water and placed it on the table in front of him. She pulled up a chair beside him and reached for his free hand, which she held to her face. "I'm some happy you came by."

Dan finished the water and slouched back in the chair, running one hand over his damp hair, the other hand over the back of Liz's hand. She wrapped her hand around his.

"Dan, I wants to ask you something. Well, I wants to tell you something, too." She looked down at their clasped hands and then up into his eyes. Her shoulders relaxed and she smiled at him. "What do you think about moving to Boston?"

He let go of her hand and pulled away.

"Let me explain, let me explain." She reached out and recaptured his hand. "Mother's sister in Boston is looking for some help with her family. Her husband's a sea captain. They have six young children. I can't stay here much longer, Dan, doing the same old thing, working now and again with the Freckers. I'm tired of living hand to mouth. I'm sick of the smell of fish."

Dan got up and moved away from her, heading for the water jug. He felt as though he hadn't had a drop to drink and his head was pounding, whether from the heat or his thoughts he couldn't tell. He filled the glass and raised it to his mouth, but was unable to drink. He put the glass down and looked at her. "People will think we're fools. Everyone came to celebrate with us, and they're expecting a wedding. We're going to build a house." He picked up the glass and threw the water out the open window.

"But, Dan, I promised Mother I'd go help Aunt Annie. We'll have a better life in Boston, we will. You'll see."

"I never said I'd go."

She got up from the table and stood in front of him, taking his arm. "Dan, it's a miserable hard life here. You knows how hard you works at the fish, you and Din. There's lots of jobs for men in Boston, too. And they pays real well. Sure, they just built an underground tunnel for the trolley cars to ride along in, Aunt Annie said. Maybe they'll build another one, and you could get a job working on it."

"Liz, I works on the ocean, not under the ground." He slipped out of her hold. "You got me in a spin. I know you talked about moving before, but I thought you were just dreaming." He shook his head. "I don't know, Liz. I don't know. Why don't we think about it after the wedding?"

"I'm going next week, Dan. Aunt Annie and them are paying for my passage."

"Next week! God save me."

"Yes, next week. You'll come down after the races." Her face was shining, and he didn't have the heart to say another word. His knees felt as wobbly as if he'd walked to her house from Cape St. Francis instead of Outer Cove. "Aunt Annie needs help. If it don't work out, we'll just come back home."

Din's cheerful face appeared around the kitchen door. "B'ys oh b'ys, it's some hot out still. Dan, me son, time to get moving. Although I can see why you'd be tempted to stay." He winked at Liz, who turned pink.

"I'll come back over after the rowing. I can't think now." Dan kissed Liz hard on the mouth and rushed out the door. His brother followed him.

"Jeez, Dan, don't you ever slow down?" The two brothers got aboard the carriage. "You looks like you're mad—or crazy." Din laughed. "And you're sweating like you just rowed a race."

"Don't laugh, Din. Wait till I tells you what Liz got on her mind."

Din snapped the reins. The afternoon sun hung over the

treetops beyond Dyer's like a giant gas lamp as they rounded Murphy's Turn and headed out the road to St. John's.

The waves on the pond rolled gently. The chilly air of spring had been driven far out to sea. In its place was a warm southwest wind which had ridden in on the Gulf Stream. The pond had awakened from its long hibernation. The boathouse was alive with young men readying shells for the year's first practice.

Watt nodded to them all, but he didn't speak. The time for gabbing was when the racing was over. Mike Snow was in his usual spot, he noted, leaning against the wood framing that supported the block and tackle for lifting the boats.

John approached Mike Snow. "Well, Snowy, how are things down in the Village? You rowing in the races this year, or are you just hanging around the pond looking for trouble?"

"No trouble around here, John. I knows what happens here on the pond during practice. It's the same old game. Crews pretend they don't see each other, and that gives them an excuse not to talk." Snowy tried to hide his brown, broken teeth as he smiled. "You're all alike.

"Torbay was out earlier this evening. Did a long row, must have been out there on the water for an hour." He spat a wad of tobacco into the pond. "They didn't look too green, that's for sure. Kind of cocky, if you ask me."

"No surprise there," Watt said. "All hands ready? Push off."

The shell moved away from the dock. The lake was calm, the boat was not. Croke seemed tense today, aggressively driving the oar deep into water, burying the blade out of sight, the water halfway up the shaft. Watt let them row for a while, hoping the boat would balance out. Then he stood up. "Everyone stop rowing." The boat drifted to a stop. "I wants you to row in pairs for a few minutes, then fours." He looked down at them, but made no eye contact. He didn't have to. Everyone knew who was causing the problem.

"The boat is rocking too much. We needs to fix that." Watt held the tiller ropes in one hand and pointed the index finger of the other at Din Croke. "Now, Croke, I wants you to watch the blade depth when John and Dan starts rowing. They'll row first." He let go of the ropes and stuck out his left arm. "Let me show you something." He looked directly at Croke. "My left arm is the water level, my right hand is the blade." He moved his right hand over and under his outstretched arm in an elliptical path. "Don't lift the oar too high out of the water on the recovery, and don't push the blade too deep on the drive. Ready, John? Ready, Dan? Show how it's done."

They started, the blades entering the pond at perfect intervals, droplets of water falling off their oars, tiny rain showers on each side of the shell. Croke watched them like an osprey spying on brown trout. He knew he had only a short time to get it right.

"On the count of two, I wants three and four to join in with five and six." Watt's coxswain's voice rang out clear over the still water. "One, two."

Croke plunged his oar into the lake, deeper than when they first left the dock. A lump was beginning to form in Watt's throat. He didn't want to single Croke out again. "Stop rowing," he shouted. "Let's try that again, but I just want three and four to row."

The crew was growing restless. Some looked up, others looked at the bank. They had been on the water ten minutes. A rocky boat, rowing in pairs, rowing in fours, and now stopping again. Mutinous murmurs ran along the inside of the shell.

"They're rowin' rough, b'ys." Clements peered around the trunk of the giant beech tree behind Summers's barn.

"Croke, is it, the man on number three?" Neddy's voice was full of scorn. "Thinks he's hauling a killick over the side."

"Look, they took in water trying to turn the boat into the breeze," Clements said, laughing. "They stinks. I believes that Croke fella is trying to kill the eels at the bottom of the pond. He got that oar buried halfway up the shaft."

"You can't get a boat moving quickly with a man like that in it." Neddy gazed at Watt's crew.

"Did he ever row in the regatta before?"

"Of course not, b'y," grunted Neddy.

"How do you know?"

"I didn't, until he pushed off the dock and took that oar in his hands."

Clements smirked. "Old Watt must be nearly cracking up."

"Slim pickings for rowers in Outer Cove this year, I suppose. If they had Jack Doran in the boat I'd be concerned, but he's not there. Them Roches and Kinsellas are rowing again, but they're no good."

"Well, if I could beat Dan McCarthy at anything, I'd think I'd died and gone to heaven." Clements ground his teeth.

"The only way to heaven with rowing is going through hell first." Neddy placed his hand on Clements's shoulder. "If that fishermen's race is close, you'll feel like hell."

Tapper and Manning, who had been silent, looked at Neddy. "You had us thinking we could beat them," Tapper said. "Now you're saying it could be close."

"I didn't say it could be close, I said *if* it's close," Neddy growled. "You boys go back to your nap."

"Watt Power can teach a monkey to row," Manning said.

"If he can't figure that Croke fella out, no one can."

"I wish they'd sink. I'd fix their boat if I could get away with it." Clements spat into the wind.

"What?" Neddy grabbed him by the shirt.

"You know, cause an accident."

"Drop that evil idea now," said Neddy, pushing him away.

"Just fooling, Neddy. Just fooling." Clements took out a pocket knife and slowly skinned the bark off a low-lying branch. The bark rolled into a coil, like the shape of a snake poised to defend itself. He grinned at the others. "Suppose we all go for a hop beer at the Happy Fisherman?"

"No. Nobody has liquor until after the races." Neddy looked into Clements's eyes. "Nobody. If you really wants to dislike someone, a certain crew, perhaps, the best thing is to give up something you likes. That will only make you dislike them more. It will also make you stronger."

"You know, that makes sense, Neddy. If they're the reason I quits having a drink for the summer, I'm going to want to beat the living daylights out of them."

Neddy grinned. "You'll enjoy the drink much more as a victor than a loser."

They slipped out past the beech and maple trees to the lane behind the boathouse. The wind had shifted to the north and become cooler. Watt's voice followed them, echoing across the pond. "Now, b'ys, let's try rowing in twos again."

Clements laughed out loud.

"No talking." Watt gazed at the bow. "Like I just said, I wants three and four to row. Everyone else, lay your blades on the water. Don't force the blade into the water, Croke. Let the weight of the oar take the blade to the water. For God's sake, did you never hear of gravity?" He sighed. Croke was in danger of breaking his oar with the force he applied to the shaft. Watt hoped no one was watching from the shore. Again, he called on them to stop rowing.

"You needs to row together, all six of ye." He lowered his voice. To show his frustration to the crew would only make them lose confidence. "Ready. Go." The boat moved forward immediately, dipping down on the stroke side. No one was at ease, but Watt was not discouraged. He had to get them some precious water time. It was only six weeks to the regatta.

The boat moved on. The other five rowers were putting on a brave face, Watt noted, but it was clear that they couldn't wait to get out of the boat. The shell continued to yaw all the way back to the dock. "Let her run." The muttering crew let go of their oars and the boat glided to the dock.

After they had gotten out of the boat, Croke moved away from the rest of the crew and grabbed his coat from the rail. He had never felt so alone in his life.

Chapter 19

Watt tossed and turned, wrestling with one thought after another. How could he get Croke to harness his powerful stroke? Keep rowing in twos? He'd tried that already. It took too much time away from all six practising together. Move him up to number five behind John, who had the perfect catch, finish? No, that would upset Dan, because he would have to move to number three oar. Get Croke closer to the cox's seat? Maybe, but that might make him even more anxious. Watt struggled to come up with a plan. Daylight was breaking, and he still hadn't slept. He got up, made some tea, and drank it. Then he went straight to John's house.

"I knows why you're here, Watt. I couldn't sleep much, either. Come in and sit down. There's no one up yet, except the birds."

"What do you think I should do with Croke, John?"

John sighed, took a deep breath, and tapped his fingers on the table. Steam rose from the teapot. Needles of blasty boughs cracked in the stove. He got up, took two slices of bread from the loaf on the counter, put them on the stove damper to toast, and then sat down again. "Let's have a mug-up and put our heads together on this."

"I can't understand it," Watt said quietly. "Nothing seems

to work with him." He placed his elbows on the table and his hands over his eyes. Croke couldn't seem to learn the catch. It seemed so simple to him and John: ease the weight of the oar when you reach ahead, in time with the other oars; put the blade in the water square to the water, like you're cutting butter. That was the catch, and Croke wasn't getting it. Watt didn't know if he should pray or cry.

John sat quietly, dipping his spoon into the cup over and over again as if he was in a trance. Watt uncovered his eyes and stared at John as he stirred his tea. He jumped up suddenly and slammed his fist down on the table. "I've got it!"

"Watt, you'll wake everyone from here to Logy Bay. Sit down, b'y." John stopped stirring. "What is it?"

"We had the same problem with young Hickey when we rowed nine twenty in the *Myrtle*. Had to get him away from rowing in the punts and skiffs for a couple of weeks." Watt's voice rose with every few words.

"Jeez, Watt. Come on, let's go out to the barn."

The two men crept across the kitchen floor to the porch, put their boots on, and went outside. The sun was opening its eye over the Rocky Hills. Two crows were cawing on an old dead spruce tree. John opened the latch to the barn door and they stepped inside. Prince swung his head around and looked at them.

"John, I just remembered Hickey telling me that the only way he could get the catch right was to stay clear of the ocean for a week or so. You knows how high those big boats are off the water compared to the shells." Watt scratched his head. "It makes sense. Croke never rowed on the pond before. He's used to hauling a load of fish through a rough sea. All he thinks about is driving the oars in, trying to get the boat through the waves."

John nodded and then looked intently at Watt. "But who's going to row for Croke when they're coming and going in the trap skiffs? He got to go fishing."

"I'll talk to his father about that, John. Will wants to see his son row in the regatta. We'll think of something."

Chapter 20

The morning sun poured through the kitchen window. Outside, the warm wind raced through the tall grass, bending and shifting it as if some giant stood above the meadow blowing with all his breath. Summer had finally taken hold in Outer Cove.

"Do you want another fish cake?" Ellen stood next to the table with the teapot. Dan's eyes seemed focused on something in front of his plate, but there was nothing to look at except the oilcloth. As for another fish cake, he had barely touched the one on his plate. She poured some tea into his half-full mug, just to get his attention. But her son continued to sit there, motionless. Only the occasional blinking of his eyes distinguished him from a corpse propped up in a chair. Ellen decided to take the bull by the horns.

"Dan, what ails you, my son?"

"Liz is going away." Dan didn't look up from the table.

"Going away? Why, where would she go? Dan, you never done nothing to her, did you?" Ellen sat down heavily in a chair on the other side of the table.

"Of course I never done nothing to her, Mother. My Jesus, this has been some year. First the tangle trying to get to the seal hunt. Then the rowing, and that cursed Din Croke. And now Liz says . . ." He took his fork and stabbed it into the half-eaten fish cake.

"Liz says what, my love?"

"She's going to Boston."

"Boston? Sacred heart of Jesus, what would she be going there for?"

"To work for her Aunt Annie Walsh."

"I suppose you'll go, too?" Ellen held her hands together as if she were about to begin a prayer. "When?" The last word was said in a whisper.

"I don't know. I can't go yet. She's leaving next week. Got her passage paid for." He shifted his chair back, rose up, went to the window, and looked out at Fitzgerald's meadow. Soft sunlight poured down the valley to the Big River. The Queen Anne's lace by the fence looked like it belonged in a bridal bouquet.

"Truth be told, if it weren't for you and Din, I'd go with her now." He turned his back to the window.

His mother's voice was so low he could barely make out her words. "What about the regatta?"

"I don't know, Mother. There's so much going on. I'm going in to John's before I goes to the beach."

He took his old black jumper off the hook on the back of the door and left. The gusting wind slapped his hair away from his brow. At the end of O'Rourke's Lane, he came face to face with Din Croke.

"Where are you going? The beach is that way." Dan pointed toward the ocean.

The younger man glanced in the direction Dan was pointing. "I'm done with going on the water for a while."

"What do you mean?"

"Didn't Watt tell you? He don't want me rowing out to the

traps for a week at least, maybe more. No rowing in the skiffs. Says it's what's making me so rough in the shells. I'm staying on shore, splitting fish." He shrugged. "Heading home for a mug-up. I'll be back down at the stage in half an hour. Suppose I'll see you at the pond this evening, if this wind drops off." He touched his cap and started to walk away.

"Wait a minute." Dan grabbed him by the sleeve. "Who's rowing in the skiff for you?"

"Watt."

Dan stood on the road, watching Din Croke's back and feeling more confused than ever. He started to walk to his house and stopped when he realized he was going in the wrong direction. There was no need to go to John's now. Watt was well on his way to fixing Croke's problems. For a moment he felt he should stay right where he was, on the road. If he went to the beach, he was going to get in a racket with the others in the crew about how bad the rowing was. If he went home, he would have to look at his mother, who was upset about his Boston talk. He sat down on the side of the road, plucked a piece of grass, and chewed on the end.

"Hello, Dan. What are you at?" Tommy Slater ducked through a gap in the longer fence and gained the road.

"Hello, young Thomas. Where are you coming from?"

Tommy raised his hand to show off two brown trout hanging from a spruce twig.

"They're grand, Tommy. You'll have them for supper, I suppose." Dan laughed.

"I can't catch them on a pole, so I set some lines in the river overnight." The boy sat down beside Dan. "I seen you walking back and forth on the road. Did you forget something on your way to the beach?"

"No, I was thinking about something. Thinking about a lot of things."

"Uncle John is always thinking, especially when Watt Power's been to the house. They're always trying to figure things out, like how to fix Din Croke's rowing." He laid the trout on top of a large rock, their mouths wide open, fins stuck against the plump bellies. The sun turned their scales into diamonds. "It's too bad Jack Doran can't row. Wouldn't be such a fuss if he was in the crew. But I wouldn't row neither if my brother was crippled and needed help at the fish."

"Dick got spina bifida. He was born with a bad spine." Dan touched Tommy on the back. "I got to go to the beach now, Tommy. You should come along. Sure, you can clean those trout down at the stage."

"Naw. I'll clean them at the house, see if Aunt Kate will let me fry them up right away. I'm some hungry."

They strolled down Slater's Hill together. "Tommy, why aren't you off swimming with the other boys on a day like this?"

"I don't like swimming. I likes to go trouting." Tommy kicked a stone. He could feel his face burning and hoped that Dan didn't see the red flush. "I got to go home now and cook me trout." He turned around abruptly and sped away like a scalded dog up Barnes Road.

"What's wrong with you, dan? I only asked a simple question." Martin stepped back.

"There's no simple goddamn questions, Martin." Dan grabbed a spool of twine. "Women aren't simple. Fishing is hard. Rowing is hard." He held the spool and let it run out until it hit the beach rocks. "What's easy about anything?"

He walked to the open door of his stage and went inside.

No comfort there, only flies competing for fish guts. Martin came in behind him.

"You got a face on you like a boiled boot. What is it?" Martin walked over to the puncheon, batted the flies away, and placed a cover over the livers.

"Me woman is moving away, away to Boston. We were supposed to marry in August. I don't know what to be doing." Dan sat down on a pile of nets. They felt good to his tired body.

"Sure, you'd go with her, wouldn't you?"

"I can't go yet, can't leave Din and Mother in the lurch. Can't leave Watt and the rest of them in the lurch, either. I wishes it was September."

"You know, Dan, my father always told me that when you're rowing on the pond and the boat is running well, all of life's problems just floats away."

"Jeez, Martin. Our boat is not running well and I got an ocean of troubles. Got any more remedies?"

"When's Liz leaving?"

"Five o'clock Monday evening." Dan looked down through the spaces in the stage floor. The tide was creeping up underneath him.

"I sees her off at Baird's Cove wharf and then goes to the pond for practice." He looked up at Martin. "Ship my woman off to the Boston States and then go for a spin on Quidi Vidi. Some life."

Martin reached down with his large hands. "Come on, Dan, b'y. Get on your feet." He pulled Dan up. "We got practice in a few hours. Let's go home, get a bit of rest. I'll pick you and Din up on the way this evening. Give Belle a break."

* * * * *

Dan had cleaned the carriage and polished Belle's harness until it shone. The afternoon sun burnished Belle's bay flanks. The solstice was past and summer was in full swing. The clear sky, the voices of the songbirds, and his spotless rig didn't help the growing emptiness in Dan's heart. The ride to Liz's seemed shorter than ever. The door to the house was open when he arrived and Liz was standing on the front steps beside a steamer trunk. She waved as he pulled up and got out of the carriage.

"Dan, Father will give you a hand to lift my trunk onto the carriage. I'll call him."

"Never mind, Liz. I can do it."

"No, Dan, it's very heavy. You wouldn't believe what I got in there. All sorts of things, including things for Aunt Annie. If you hurt your back, Watt will come down to Boston after me."

Dan sat down on the trunk and pulled Liz to him. He felt sick. He couldn't say anything, so he moved to kiss her. A man's voice said, "Hello, my son." Dan jumped to his feet, and the two men shook hands.

"Good day, Mr. Malone."

"You ready to take her out to town? I hates to see her go, but what can we do? She's a smart girl, knows there's more of a future for the two of ye in Boston. Mind you gets down there quick before some Yankee snaps her up." Pat Malone turned to his daughter. "Where's your mother, Liz?"

"She's in the bedroom on her knees with the rosary. She's reeling off novenas like they're going out of style, praying the ship won't run into a hurricane. I'll go get her." Liz turned and headed into the house. When she got to her parents' bedroom, she slowly opened the door. "Mother, Dan is here. I'm going now."

Sadie Malone looked up from where she knelt by the white wrought-iron bedstead. Her face was swollen, her eyes red. She blinked once and then picked up the end of her apron and wiped away the tears running down her face.

"I'm going to miss you some bad, Mother." Liz knelt beside her.

"I'm going to miss you, too, my darling." The rosary beads fell from Sadie's hands as she reached out to hold her daughter in her arms. "You better save your money and come back home to visit. You, Dan, and your youngsters." She drew in a long, shuddering breath and bit her lip, trying to hold back another flood of tears.

Mother and daughter gently rocked together on the mat Sadie had finished hooking in February. It was beautiful, but not thick enough to keep the cold of the wood floor out of their knees. After a while, Liz could feel her mother stop sobbing. Her own face was wet with tears.

"You knows I'll come back, Mother. Boston isn't halfway around the world." She helped Sadie to her feet, and they tidied themselves up, wiping each other's eyes.

"I'm a right mess, Liz."

"Me too, Mother. But I have to go now."

"I know, child, I know."

When she saw the towers of the Basilica in the distance, Liz moved closer to Dan. The ship that would take her away from him was just past those towers and down over the hill in the harbour.

"Are you going to write to me, Liz?"

"Of course I'm going to write to you. Every week, more often if I got lots of news. Are you going to answer my letters, Dan?"

"Yes, I suppose I can write a few lines." He laughed, took the reins in one hand, and put his other arm around her, bringing her close.

"How's Din Croke making out with the rowing since he stopped going out to the traps?" Liz nestled into Dan.

"I didn't think you thought that much about the rowing, Liz."

"Everybody in Outer Cove, Middle Cove, and Logy Bay thinks about the rowing." She kissed him gently on the side of his face. "I'll miss going to the races. You better win. You better win it all." She reached across and squeezed his hand.

The bright sun softened the hardness of the old town. Liz wondered if it might be the last time she would ever see it. It had all been so sudden, so rushed, her engagement to Dan and then the decision to move away. Was it the right decision? There was no time to wonder about that. They were on Ordnance Street, and she could see the stacks and masts of ships.

"I think I'll tie Belle on here at Neal's. We'll walk to the dock. Too many people to take the carriage any closer," said Dan. He pulled up in front of the brick building, got out of the carriage, and tied the mare to a ring projecting from a wall. Liz followed him.

"Who's going to lug the chest to the ship?"

"We are. You grab one handle and I'll get the other. Come on, Liz, the two of us can do it. Sure, just think of all the things you'll have to lift and haul after we gets married. Youngsters, for instance." He smiled at the blush slowly staining her cheeks.

"Dan McCarthy, you been hanging around Watt Power too long. You're always thinking about an easier way to move or lift something." She grinned at him and then reached down and took one of the handles of the trunk.

They inched their way along to the dock, stopping frequently. Finally, they reached the ship and sat down on a bollard, side by side. Dan glanced at Liz out of the corner of his eye, at her new straw hat and the strong profile beneath it. She looked like a queen. He spoke quickly, to keep the lump out of his throat. "Got your ticket?"

"Yes." She opened her purse and showed it to him. As she closed the bag, the ship's horn blasted. It was time to board. She and Dan got to their feet.

"You'll come to Boston after the races, won't you?" She put her arms around him.

"Yes, Liz, I will. Right after the races, I'll come to Boston."

"I got to go aboard now, Dan." She buried her face in his shoulder. "I loves you."

He held her so tight he thought he might break her bones, but she didn't move.

Reluctantly, they let go of each other. Two longshoremen took the trunk on board, and Liz followed it. Eventually, the gangway disappeared, and the massive ropes that moored the steamer were untied, the anchor weighed.

Liz was at the rail, waving to him. He waved back, looking at her until her face was only a small white blur. The *Dartmouth* sounded its horn for the final time and steered toward the Narrows, finally disappearing into the fog that was licking at the rocky ledges of Fort Amherst.

The ride from the harbour to the pond seemed almost not to have happened. One minute he was holding Liz in his arms, the next it was as if he'd been kicked out of a dream. The carriage was passing the hospital on Forest Road before he realized where he was. He glanced at the pond, shining on the other side of the leafy poplar trees. There was no saying to the crew that he couldn't row today. He would have to get in the boat and leave his heartache on the dock.

They were waiting in the shell when he arrived. No one said a word to him as he got in and strapped his feet into the footing. As the boat sailed out onto the waters of Quidi Vidi, Dan thought of Liz's ship steaming out of the harbour. Then he put all thoughts of her away.

"It's a grand day for a row," said Watt. "Keep the stroke long."

The crew settled into the spin, fully focused. "Now, men," Watt said, "keep your head in the boat. No looking around. Feel the boat move away from the water. You will make this boat move away from the water." His voice had a hypnotic quality that helped them push themselves mentally and physically.

"You can only be in pain when the race is over. And if you wins, there's no pain." Watt was good at keeping bad thoughts away, reflected Dan. He knew how hard they worked, and for no wages. It was for the sport and for their pride.

"That's excellent, Croke. Keep that blade just under the surface of the water. You have it now, the catch that you need." Watt's experiment with Croke had worked. The boat was balanced. His praise for Croke affected Dan and the rest of the crew, unravelling the thread of doubt that had undermined their earlier efforts. Croke's powerful stokes had been harnessed—the boat was balanced and fast.

"Now, men, let's work on the recovery. All hands, the same level. Keep the blades the same height off the water." Croke wasn't holding back. His blade sent waves of water toward the tiller. Dan watched the wash go by. He rowed harder, not wanting to be shown up by the new man in the boat.

"Another five minutes and we'll call her quits. You knows the rate we're rowing. One hundred and twenty strokes to go, equal pressure on each one." Watt's voice dismissed all thoughts of quitting. The shell skimmed across the pond, the hull cutting through the water like a shark's fin.

"Seven strokes to the finish. Bring the rate up." The force of the boat moving forward pushed Watt's back into the rear of the seat. He gripped the tiller ropes to keep himself stable as the boat increased in speed. "Let her run." The boat glided to a stop and the crew leaned on their oars, catching their breath.

Watt stood up and addressed them. "A good row, men. Twenty minutes without stopping. Good balance most of the time, good pressure on the blades all the time. Pressure on the blades, that's what makes her go."

Dan dipped his hand in the cool pond to ease the burning of his flesh. He was almost too tired to think. Through the haze of the fatigue and pain, he managed one thought of Liz, somewhere out on the ocean. Was she thinking of him? He pulled his hand out of the water. It felt better. He put both hands back on the oars and rowed with the rest of the crew to the dock, with Watt still standing in the stern. They disembarked.

"Tomorrow, same time," Watt called to the retreating figures of his crew. "We'll walk out to the pond from the cove together."

"What? Walk out from the cove?" Croke's voice was an octave higher than usual.

"Never mind, Croke, b'y," said Nugent. "Old Watt will get us a ride home. You'll need one." He slapped Croke on the back.

"Dan, what's wrong with you? You're not yourself." Din grabbed a big, gutted fish by the tail and tossed it on the splitting table. Its bones cracked when he separated the head from the thick body on the edge of the table. "Maybe you needs to see a doctor." He shoved the fish across the splitting table to Dan.

"I don't need to see no goddamn doctor." Dan took the knife and ran the blade along the two sides of the backbone on the inside of the fish. He repeated the cut on the outside, then removed the bone, letting it fall through a hole in the stage floor onto the beach rocks below. "I don't need no doctor. I don't know what I needs. Maybe I'm just fed up." He stuck the bloody knife in the table.

"We're having a good year at the fish. The crew is coming along. What's there to complain about?" Din dipped the split fish into the water barrel to clean it.

"Did you hear me complain? Did you?" Dan moved until he was within inches of Din, then turned around and picked up a handful of salt and threw it at the wall. "You don't understand, you don't. Your woman is here in the cove, isn't she? You can see her moving around in her yard out the window of our house." He kicked the water barrel over, sending fish spewing over the stage floor, and strode toward the door. "The hell with this racket."

A light drizzle drifted into the cove and carried the salty sea air up the valley in tiny drops that barely wet the grass that had grown tall in the meadows. The seed pods on the hay crop drooped under the weight of the damp air and their own weight. Fog tumbled down over the Rocky Hills, stopping at the edge of the road.

"What a mauzy old day. I hates the thought of rowing on a day like this. You ready to go? We got to meet John down at the end of the lane. Then we'll get Croke on the way out the road. You knows this is the first day we walks to the lake before we rows?"

Dan turned away from the window and nodded. "Yes, Din, I knows. Walk for an hour and a half, then row."

Din took a bottle, filled it with water, and pushed a cork in the top. He put on his coat and hat, taking his time, casting glances at his brother. Finally, he said, "You coming?"

"Yes, I suppose," Dan mumbled.

"Come on, b'y, nothing like a good walk with your buddies to clear your head." Din put his arm around Dan's shoulders, then pushed him away.

"I don't need to walk for five miles to clear my noggin." Dan grinned for what seemed the first time in days.

"Let's go, Dan. I can see John coming up over Slater's Hill."

The mist on the pond helped keep them cool as Watt drilled them through short, intense rows. Four minutes of rowing at race pace and three minutes' rest. They knew they had to do this five times before the practice ended. The day seemed to go on forever, but at last the spin ended. They tied the boat to the dock, too tired to talk.

"How do all of us get home?" asked Croke. He was barechested, trying to wring the sweat out of his shirt.

"Don't worry, Croke," said Watt. "Neighbours are better than friends." No sooner had he spoken than Pat Griffin and Mike Kelly rode up to the boathouse with their horses and long carts. "There you go. Hop aboard one of those rigs and you'll be home before dark."

"Is there anything that man won't do to keep his crew together?" said Dan.

"Watt keeps ahead of everyone," said John as he climbed

aboard Mike's cart and sat next to him. "If one plan don't work, he thinks of a new one. Mike, how are you getting on? Here comes Martin and Nugent. You'll have a full load of manure to drag back to the cove with you today."

"I'm best kind," said Mike. "I suppose the rowing's going good? I can't wait for to see the races."

The crew's weary legs dangled over the sides of the two carts. Dan's back ached, but the long, rough ride was better than walking back. The sun had almost set. His mother would be looking out the window for him and Din. He was glad the day's work was over. Watt would say a proper day's work was spending the day fishing and the evening rowing, but Dan couldn't agree with that. Some days, perhaps.

The carts pulled to a stop. John, Dan, and Din got off and began to walk down O'Rourke's Lane on aching legs. Their tired bodies cast shadows of giants as the sun dipped into the treetops beyond Pine's farm.

"That was a fine row this evening," said John. "We're coming together, b'ys. I seen the wash from the blades run well past the rudder this evening."

"Do you think we're getting good distance on the drive, John?" asked Din.

"Not entirely. We're getting better, but the boat is slow during the longer rows. We needs to do more of those. Water time is everything now. Extra time on the pond will get the boat up to speed. We'll just keep working hard. Watt will keep us up to the mark."

Dan and Din stopped at the gate of their house. Din untied the rope that held it shut. John stopped, too, and leaned on the fence for a moment. The hard day was done.

.

Chapter 21

As the men worked the trap, gulls swooped and dived around the skiff, hoping to scavenge any fish that may have slipped away from the haul. The cod flipped and squirmed on the surface of the trap. The dip nets buckled under the weight of the fish as the crew hauled them aboard.

The boat was filled to the gunwales before the sun had crested the cliffs at Torbay Point. John's empty stomach growled. He could see the grey puffs of smoke rising from his chimney. It was a short season at the trap fishery. Like the races, it was intensely difficult. In both cases, hopes were simple: a decent price for the catch and victory at the regatta. The crew was tossing two sets of dice at two different tables. Fish or die. Win at the races or lose the cove's pride of place.

Kate wiped the table and placed the fresh bread on it. "You were tossing and turning like a fish out of water last night. Is it your back that's acting up again? Maybe you should see a doctor."

"I've never seen a doctor and I don't suppose I'll ever see one unless you gets a doctor to come in when I'm dying." John leaned back in the chair and ran his hand through his sweat-soaked hair. "That'll be soon enough, I guess."

"Now, John, don't say that. You're not old." She took a knife out of the drawer and sharpened it on the whetstone. "You're able to do everything the younger men in the crew are doing." She cut the loaf into thick slices. "What kept you from sleeping sound last night? God knows you were tired enough when you went to bed. If it isn't your back, it must be your mind." She put salt fish and pieces of pork fat in the hot frying pan. "Are you worried about the crew? John, I wish you'd give up the rowing, or at least give up thinking about it . . ."

The smell and the sound of the fish and the fat cooking stalled John's thinking. He could put up with a sore back if he could only figure out how to increase the speed of the boat.

"I'll throw in a couple of eggs for you to have with your fish and brewis. It's the last of the eggs this week from Dowden's. We'll have to get more hens soon." Kate's old hens had not lasted the winter.

John's mouth watered. He dug into his breakfast. The fish, the salted butter, the eggs, the brewis, and bread tasted as if he were eating them for the first time. He finished his tea and rose quickly from the table, barely able to conceal the shooting pain in his back. "I got to get back to the beach. We'll be heading out to the trap again this afternoon. Twice a day while the fish are inshore."

"You can rise from that chair without pain. You're not too bad off, then."

"I'm fine, Kate. We landed a lot of fish this morning. Guess you'll be down to the flake the once with Tommy." He blessed himself and started for the door. "Got a spin on the pond at six. Come get me after you sells the bum of fish and gets clear of the shops." He kissed her and slipped way.

The warm wind lifted the curtain hanging at the open window. Tommy came in, bright-eyed, his cheeks flushed.

"Aunt Kate, the caplin are rolling. Where's Uncle John?"

"You must have missed him. He's gone to the beach. Well, now we'll have to get the buckets and go out after the caplin, won't we?" said Kate. "And then we'll bury them in the garden. But first, you needs something in your belly. Come sit down, I gets you a feed of fish and brewis."

The splashing of the cool water against John's face felt good. He took the wet shaving brush and rubbed it into the soap. The sun's reflection off the razor blade danced against the bedroom ceiling. He made careful, wide swipes across his face, removing the speckled stubble, then wiped his face and neck clean. The shadows of age vanished. He combed his hair and stared at his reflection in the mirror above the washstand. Then he gave a snort and turned and headed down to the kitchen. Kate was out in the garden with Tommy; he wouldn't disturb her. He got himself a plate of fish and bread, spreading the bread with butter and the thick blueberry preserve Kate had made last summer. His back didn't feel as sore as it had that morning. He hoped that the evening practice wouldn't make it worse.

The westerly breeze slowly drifted down from the Ross farm and spread across the water, creating a slight headwind as they rowed up the pond. It gave the crew a chance to cool; Watt had been relentless with his calling. He and John had decided that more time on the water would help the crew improve its speed. Today, the spin seemed to go on forever. It was a dizzying ordeal, and the men found it hard to conceal their pain. John could tell the run in the boat was improving, but time was getting short. They had only a few weeks to improve their speed. Nugent had begun to complain that some of the spins were too long, that the men were getting more blisters than usual. The boat's speed was not what John was used to—it was less than it should be. What was the remedy? They needed to change something. He got out of the shell slowly and went to the boathouse with the rest of them.

"We need to meet at the liver house on Sunday," said Watt, leaning against the rail, filling his pipe with tobacco. "There's time left to improve, but you got to want to get better."

The crew sat with their backs along the boathouse wall, their exhausted faces looking up at Watt. John let his gaze drift away across the pond. He was tired and his body hurt. He got up and walked out of the boathouse to the public well beside the penitentiary wall, put his head under the spout, and pumped the water over him, drinking it as it ran by his mouth. He drank until his body felt cooler, and then he sat down on the grassy bank. Leaning back, he watched the clouds tumble in the sky above him. He closed his eyes.

"John Whelan. Mr. Whelan, is that you? Are you all right, man?"

There were spots in his eyes. John blinked to clear his vision. He searched for the voice and saw a grand carriage tackled up to a chestnut mare a few feet away. *I must have fallen asleep*, he thought. A man was sitting in the carriage. There was a black bag at his feet. John shook his head and leapt to his feet.

"Dr. Rendell, sir. I was waiting for my wife to come by and take me home. We were rowing." He walked over to the carriage, reached up, and shook the doctor's hand.

"How's the rowing? Not much time left before the big day."

"We're working hard. Real hard, but we can't seem to get a good run in the boat at the end of the spins."

"I hear Torbay is rowing some quick times in practice. So says Sissy Snow, our parlour maid. I do believe her brother has an interest in the races."

Sissy Snow—she was Mike Snow's sister. John arched his body to stretch his frame. He grimaced.

"Have you hurt your back?"

"No, sir, not really. Traps have been full lately. I've been doing a lot of hauling." John shrugged. "It's nothing, sir. We just rowed around the pond twice, with no breaks."

"Why don't you come and see me at the hospital tomorrow? I'll have a look at you, just a quick exam. No charge."

John's face felt stiff. "I'm not sick or nothing, Dr. Rendell. You don't have to bother with me."

"Trust me, John, I'm not going to poke at you. Not much, anyway. Let's say five o'clock. Try to get some rest this evening." The doctor smiled reassuringly at John, then clucked to his mare and turned her onto Boathouse Lane. He quickly disappeared up the steep incline sheltered by lush maples.

"Try to get some rest this evening." John grinned. He had animals to tend to and a trap lead to mend. Perhaps he could put the lead off for one more day. There was too much at stake now, and he knew his body wasn't right.

There were the poor, the very poor, and the ones no one cared about at all. Where did these people get enough food to eat? Kate wondered. They had no farms, no gardens. She directed Prince toward Water Street and its many shops, away from the slums of Carter's Hill and Haggerty Street with its unpainted shacks and unkempt children. She said a short prayer as she drove Prince away from the stink of the gutters in the summer heat, the rancid odour no longer subdued by colder temperatures.

A fine layer of coal dust hung over the west end, a layer of filth above the city. She was looking forward to getting out of it all, to heading east to the lake to get her husband, and then going home to the blessed country.

"John, if you're going to see Dr. Rendell, you'd better get cleaned up, my son, and I mean cleaned up." Kate stood in front of him with a towel and a bar of lye soap. "You'd best head down to the Big River and have a wash. Unless you wants me to haul out the tub."

"I know, I know. I'm heading to the river now." He grinned. "I'll be as clean as a christening babe when I gets back, don't you worry." He took the towel and soap from her and walked to the porch.

"I got to go over to me sister's for a bit. What time will you be home?"

"I don't know for sure. Probably about eight o'clock."

The cold touch of the stethoscope made John flinch. Dr. Rendell moved the device around his torso, his face expressionless. Then he removed the stethoscope's earpieces and took John's wrist, holding the index and second finger of the other hand against it while he looked at his watch. He raised his eyebrows. "Turn over on your stomach, please."

John lay on his stomach while the doctor probed his back from buttocks to shoulders and along each side of the spine. He made a bow of his body in response to the pain when the doctor's fingers pressed the soreness.

"You may get dressed now, Mr. Whelan. It seems your lower back is strained." Dr. Rendell sat down in his chair and stretched his arms. "Otherwise, you're in very good health. In fact, I'm quite sure you have an athlete's heart. Your resting heart rate is forty beats per minute. Mine is seventy, which is normal."

John wasn't sure what to say. The hospital was such a foreign place, and the doctor's examination had unsettled him. But he was curious. "What do you mean, sir, an athlete's heart?"

"I remember our conversation when you brought the young Cahill girl here in the winter storm. You said that when you rowed, the effort didn't seem like work to you." Dr. Rendell crossed his arms and leaned back in his chair.

"That's how I felt before my back started acting up."

"At the lake yesterday, you said that the boat was not getting the run you think it should be getting, especially toward the end of the spins."

"That's right, sir. I can tell by the distance the wash from number two's oar travels as it passes by the rudder. I've seen thousands of strokes go by me on number six. We're not holding our speed. We're not getting the distance." John buttoned his shirt.

"When I was at school, I was a runner. The mile, actually. But I really didn't like it. I couldn't train like the others, who ran four, sometimes five miles each evening. They had to do that to build up their endurance to run a shorter distance faster. Athletes who train for distance events have to work hard over a much longer distance than that of the event they are training for." He rose from his chair, took the stethoscope from around his neck, put it on the desk, and sat down beside it.

"Don't let this go to your head, Mr. Whelan, but you're an exception to the rule, physically. There are, however, five other men rowing that boat. It's the overall strength and endurance of the crew that will determine if you win or lose." He glanced at his watch.

"What do you suppose we have to do to get the boat up to speed, Dr. Rendell?"

"It's quite simple. I think you know the answer."

"Longer rows?"

"Yes, longer rows. You all know how to row. What you need is to improve your wind and your muscular strength." He shook hands with John and opened the office door for him. "Your back should be fine with a few days' rest."

"I don't get much rest, sir."

"You'll get less rest if you do longer rows. But sometimes you have to work with pain, as you know. Depends on how much the rowing means to you. Good luck with it, Mr. Whelan."

How would they get the long rows in, and where? Was it worth it? John went to the stable to get his horse. He had the five-mile ride back to Outer Cove in which to plan the next twenty days. He wished it were fifty miles.

Tommy stroked Prince's mane and tried to coax him to eat the carrot he'd sneaked out of the bin, but the horse turned his head away, breathing heavily. "Come on, boy, have the carrot. You likes carrots." The boy watched, perplexed, as Prince hung his head and started kicking at his belly. He suddenly sank onto the grass and let out a groan.

"Tommy, do you know where John is?" Kate shouted through the pantry window at the boy, who was in Prince's pound.

"I believes he's at the beach mending the trap," Tommy called back.

"Go on down and tell him I have to go out of the house for a few hours."

"I'll go now, Aunt Kate." Tommy raced off down through

the meadow, running as hard as he could until he reached John, who was working under the stage.

"Uncle John," he cried out, trying to catch his breath. "Aunt Kate sent me to tell you she's got to leave the house for a while. But there's something else, too." He held on to one of the stage posts to steady himself. "Prince is acting strange. He wouldn't eat the carrot or drink the water I took him. He's lying down, and he don't look good. His eyes are queer." John dropped the mending needle, which fell on the beach rocks. He left the stage, with Tommy following close behind. As he approached the house, he saw the horse on his side in the pound.

"What's wrong with him, Uncle John?" Tommy whispered. "Did a bee bite his belly?"

John shook his head. He climbed the fence and dropped down into the enclosure. Prince lay stretched out, his sides heaving. John knelt beside him, running his hands over the horse's bloated stomach. Then he got up and climbed back over the fence and went in the house. Tommy was standing beside the stove, white-faced.

"Are you going to have to shoot him?" The boy's voice was full of cracks.

John put his arm around Tommy. "Now, young Thomas, don't go worrying yourself. I won't harm Prince. I'm not sure what's wrong. Maybe it's something he ate. I needs to go to Middle Cove and see Phil Kinsella, he knows a lot about horses. Sure, he's a seventh son of a seventh son, he can cure anything on legs. You come with me." There was no time to contemplate fish, rowing, or anything else. He took Tommy by the hand and left the house.

* * * * *

Tommy held on tightly to Kate's arm. They were looking out the window at John and Phil Kinsella, who had managed to get Prince to his feet. The horse was tied to the fence, his head sagging.

"What are they going to do to him, Aunt Kate?"

"They got to get some mineral oil into his stomach, to make him better." She patted the top of the shaggy head beside her.

The horse screamed as the two men placed the tube in his mouth. Tommy covered his ears. Kate felt his small body tremble. She gathered him to her.

"Prince will be all right, Tommy. Uncle John and Mr. Kinsella knows what they're doing."

A large moth, drawn by the bright glow of the kerosene light, cast a dancing shadow on the tin ceiling of the kitchen. It fluttered its wings at the warm lamp, fell back, and started the whole process over again. Kate sat knitting next to the cool stove. The sound of the rockers on her chair barely broke the silence. John lay on the daybed, exhausted, his body in the same position as it was when he first lay down after Phil Kinsella left. A warm wind whistled in through the slightly raised window.

"John, can you hear me?" Kate said quietly. He stirred, shifted his body, and opened his eyes.

"Heavenly Father, what time is it? I must have drifted off."

"You been sleeping for three hours." She got up and laid the needles and yarn on the table. "You go on up to bed. I'll put the light out and come right up behind you."

The half moon in the clear summer sky trickled a small, dull light across the bedroom floor. The mattress was warm and soft beneath John's tired body. He had walked Prince for hours up and down the field until the horse was out of danger. As exhausted as he was, there was still tension in his whole body from Prince's brush with death. Colic could kill a horse as quick as that. Thank God for Phil Kinsella.

"What did Dr. Rendell have to say, John?" Kate blew out the candle on the night table.

"He said my back is just a bit sore, that's all. It's not me back that's bothering me, Kate, it's that man's idea of how to make the boat go faster." He reached his arm out and pulled her closer. "I'm too tired to explain. We got a crew meeting tomorrow evening." He picked up her warm hands and closed his eyes. "I'll tell you after the meeting, if there's not some kind of mutiny against Watt." He sighed deeply. "If you got the windows of the house open, you'll probably hear the yelling."

Chapter 22

John whispered soothingly to Prince as he stroked the horse's back and sides with the curry comb.

"That damn colic." John turned around. Watt was standing just inside the barn. "I lost a good mare to it once."

John motioned with his head toward the house. "Let's go up and have a cup of tea. Tommy and Kate are gone to church, for Benediction."

Watt grinned. "Maybe we should have gone, too. A few prayers might get us back on the pond a bit quicker."

John grinned back at him and the two men left the barn. When they got inside the house, John put some water in the kettle and laid it on the stove. "I was talking with Dr. Rendell after our row on Wednesday. He's some clever, that man."

"Yes, b'y, he is." Watt sat down and pulled his chair closer to the table.

"Remember what Sexton said about him last fall?" John leaned ahead on his chair. "He said the man knows about a lot of things. Well, Dr. Rendell told me something I suppose I always knew, but I didn't pay much attention to it."

The kettle whistled. John placed the loose, coarse tea in the pot and filled it with boiling water. "He asked me how the crew was shaping up, and I told him. I said that we weren't happy with the way the boat was running. He said we needs to muscle up, get our second wind. How do you suppose we're going to do that? We're already walking to the pond three times a week, and rowing, too."

"That's what we got to figure out this evening, John. I'm not losing a regatta to Torbay."

"Torbay rowed nine twenty in practice yesterday. That might get the crew on the go." John looked out the window. "The McCarthys are coming down Slater's Hill. We'll have to skip the tea. Time to visit the stinky hut!"

Watt and John were the last to file in. Five long faces stared at them. Watt didn't keep them waiting.

"Men," he began, "I knows Quidi Vidi well. I knows the shore and the winds." He took a gaff from the wall and held it out in front of him. "John knows the number of strokes it takes to get a boat from point to point around the pond. I knows the time it takes."

He measured each step across the floor, jabbing the gaff into the rough wood as he walked. Then he raised it up and drove it into a beam. A loud thud echoed through the building.

"We needs to get in better shape or risk losing." He kicked open the liver house door and pointed at the beach. "We're going to row from there to Logy Bay every second day in a trap skiff, starting tomorrow."

Nugent jumped to his feet. "You'll row there without me."

"Me, too," said Dan quickly. The place fell silent, save for the trickle of water beneath the floor.

"Are you men, or aren't you?" said Watt.

"I think you've gone cracked," Dan shot back. "Me hands

and arse are sore enough now. If we do row, what do we row in? You can't put a racing shell on the sea." The others laughed.

"Laugh if you wants," said John, "but Torbay rowed nine twenty yesterday."

"How do you know that?" asked Nugent.

Watt tapped John on the shoulder. "Tell them how you found out."

"Snowy told me. You all knows him—he don't make up stories." John looked at each of them. "They rowed last evening. Stake one, a perfect pond, about an hour after we finished. They had stopwatches. It's no secret."

"Tell them about the new boat, John," Watt urged.

"I don't want to hear about the new boat. How would rowing from here to Logy Bay make us better?" Dan stood up quickly, almost hitting his head on the low ceiling.

"Dr. Rendell," John said. "The man who designed Bob Sexton's new boat. He's taken an interest in this crew. Don't ask me why, but I trusts him and what he says. He knows how your body works, and how you can make it perform better." The others sat still, listening. "You knows yourself you can't row for a long time at the beginning of the season. You got to work yourself up to it. Rendell says we got to go longer and harder."

"We've always rowed the same. Why the hell do we have to change now?" demanded Nugent.

"Torbay has rowed nine twenty, Jack." Watt stepped into the centre of the floor. "If they better that time Regatta Day and we're not faster, they'll own the course record. Do you want them to get that record, the record Outer Cove has held for sixteen years?"

He closed the open door. "Here's something else to think about. Consider the time it takes to get to the pond—you knows, walking or driving—and the practice itself. That's three hours out of every day." He searched his jumper pocket for a match. "We can row from here to Logy Bay in less than an hour and a half, and then you're finished."

"How do we get home from Logy Bay?" asked Boland. "I'm not bloody walking."

Watt struck a match off the grindstone. He took a deep draw on his pipe, puffing until a blue haze clouded his face. "The Logy Bay people will help us. They'll get us home."

The rows on the pond after the meeting seemed like a new beginning. Practice by practice, the boat became a little faster. John didn't look as often at the wash of the oars going by. The shortness and intensity of the practices seemed to invigorate the crew. On the pond, there was no tide, no miles of swells to make them weary. John now had to play close attention to his catch, adjusting its quickness as the boat speed quickened. He and Dan seemed to be connected at the hip, and also at the brain, when it came to the pace they had to set for the four behind them. Brief words were sometimes exchanged between John and Dan when they were in the shell. When Croke asked why they were allowed to talk in the boat, Boland told him they had their own private language and it was none of his business. John knew Watt didn't know and didn't care what he and Dan said to each other. In past races, despite the pressure, the pain, the sweating, and the sideways glances, he and Dan had always had a word or two for each other.

Watt sat at the rear of the skiff during every row the crew made on the ocean. He called those rows "the journey around Torbay Point." It was either a journey from Outer Cove to Logy Bay or the reverse. He never omitted the name of a single landmark, be it a shoal or fishing berth. Like a good skipper, Watt praised the crew's dedication to the three-mile rows. He also condemned the Torbay crew roundly and loudly, which made them row all the harder. "We'll give them their fill of rowing! That nine twenty won't be quick enough to beat us."

"Here comes the crew from Outer Cove!" Children came running down from the fishing rooms to the cliff's edge.

"I seen them first," said Kitty Burke.

"No, you never, I did," said her brother, watching the crew, covered in spray, pound headlong into the stiff westerly breeze, their backs bent to take on the last fifteen minutes against a headwind.

"Push to finish, men—I can see the chimneys in Dyer's Cove." Watt brought them in to land beneath the cliffs at Logy Bay. Wet and worn out, they tied up the boat to a ladder that led up the cliff face.

"Come have a mug-up, now, fellas, before we takes you back to Outer Cove. You must be nearly all in." Pat Malone walked the men up to his fishing room, where there was fresh meat stew waiting. They sat outside on the soft moss, flanked by berry bushes, and ate.

"Mr. Malone, have you heard from Liz yet?" asked Dan.

"No, not yet, my son. Been almost two weeks now, though I don't have to tell you that. I expects we'll get a letter from her soon." He offered the men more bread to sop up the stew, and fresh tea. "Not long till the races now, b'ys. Just a dozen or so days left."

"The boat is setting up well," Dan said, "but I've had enough of practising." He spat a wad of tobacco into the grass and looked at the children playing where Liz played when she was a child, in a tiny corner at the edge of the sea. The lush green hills of Cadigan's Side swept down to the fish flakes. Shafts of golden sunlight shone through breaks in the racing white clouds.

"Pining for me daughter, are you, Dan, b'y?" Pat Malone gave Dan a good-natured shove. "Eat up, you needs your strength. Liz won't be too happy with you if you loses to Torbay on Regatta Day."

"Who wants to ride back to Outer Cove with me?" Willy Cadigan shouted.

"Meself and young Croke will climb aboard with you, Willy," said Watt.

Up the steep incline of the Rooms Road they went.

"When do you think we'll row for time, Watt?" Croke asked.

"Don't worry, my son. The new boat Sexton built is getting christened today. We'll take her for a spin this evening. She will be quick. She got to be. If she's really slick, we'll need to get used to her. And she got to get used to the water. All that new wood needs to be primed up. We're pretty smooth. I'd say that next week we'll be the first crew going for a poke in that boat."

"Going for a poke? What do you mean?"

"We're going to row for time. Take a poke at the record set in 1885. You know, the nine twenty that Torbay matched in practice last week." Watt took his stopwatch out of his breast pocket and dangled it in front of Croke and the rest of the crew.

"Why can't we row for time in the *Glance* today? Could be windy next week. You know what it took to row nine twenty. What do you remember?"

"There was a slight tailwind as we were rowing down the

pond, but we pushed hard, knowing the same wind would help us on the way home."

"So you had a good turn?"

"An excellent turn. My father was a damn good coxswain on the buoy. It was the fisherman's race, a dandy four-boat race. At least that's what we thought before the starter's gun fired. It was never close. We rowed for time. We rowed away from them." Watt pushed his hand through the air as if batting a fly. "Maybe that's why we were so fast. Because we knew right away we were going to win. It did our hearts good."

Croke moved closer to Watt. "Did you know how fast you were before you finished?"

"No, we never. We never give it no thought, we were too busy rowing. A race goes by that fast. Before you knows it, you're starting to turn, and that's about four minutes, thirty. Then all of a sudden you're back to where the Virginia River comes into the pond. Just three minutes to go." He grinned. "You hurt like hell and you've rowed about six minutes then."

"You was beat out by then?" Croke said.

Watt's hands were gesturing like an Italian's. "Yes, but you can't stop. You're in a boat with six other men. You can't let them down." He took Croke's hand and squeezed it. "You can't let the people of the cove down, or your family, or all the people on the banks of the pond. You'd rather die than quit."

"Don't you suffer like a martyr?"

"Some do and some don't." Watt paused, and looked at Croke's young, eager face. "Suffering is a great teacher, my son."

Dan had been counting the days since Liz left, and the days remaining for him in the cove. The fishery had slowed down, but the first hay crop had to be cut and dried. The gardens needed tending, and there were always repairs, at home and at the stage. They were rowing six days a week: Monday in the skiff to Logy Bay, Tuesday on the pond, Wednesday in the skiff from Logy Bay back to Outer Cove, Thursday on the pond, and so on, until it ended on Saturday. Dan and the rest of them wished for a gale so they could get a break, but so far the winds had stayed away.

It was a week before the races when he returned home from the beach to find an envelope on the kitchen table.

"I was going by Dyer's and they told me there was a piece of mail for you," called Din from his bedroom.

Dan's heart raced as he sat down at the table and carefully peeled the flap open.

July 19, 1901
Boston, Mass.

My Darling Dan,
It is twelve days since I arrived in Boston. I've been very busy, and that has helped keep me from thinking of you and my parents too much. I hope you are good. I misses you terribly, Dan. Aunt Annie's children are ages one to eight, and they all seems to want me at the same time. But the Walshes are very good to me. Their house is some grand. They even got a bathroom, with a big porcelain tub! I was afraid to get in it first, it's so deep, but now I gets in twice a week.

I took a ride on the subway one Sunday. It's very fast. I likes the streetcars better. There's some lot to see here. Aunt Annie takes me around with her when she can, and I goes by myself on Sundays, which is my day off. It's a lonely day for me, walking around the streets of Boston wishing you was with me.

I have met a lot of people from home who moved here and are happy to stay. They mostly lives in the same spot and they visits each other all the time. I asked them all to our wedding—you better come down soon!

I wish I had got a picture of you, but the only one I ever seen is in the front room of your house and I know your mother wanted to hang on to that.

Please write to me soon. I am hoping you knows when you will be coming to Boston. That way I can mark off the days on the little calendar Aunt Annie give to me. (It got roses on the front of it, like the ones I wants for my bouquet.)

All my love,
Liz (Star of Logy Bay)
P.S.—Beat Torbay in the races!

Watt decided that the last long row would be one week before the regatta. The crew would spend any extra time practising starts, turning the buoys, and, if there was a good pond, rowing for time. The extra rowing in the skiff had paid off. Torbay wanted the *Red Cross*; Sexton's new shell was theirs to row. The *Blue Peter* cut through the water the way Sexton said it would, with little resistance.

"Who's that, I wonder?" Din got up from the table in response to the sound of boots crossing the yard. The porch door was pushed open.

"Come in, come in, Croke, b'y. I'm having a feed of toutons. Hang on, now, till I gets you a plate." Din filled a plate with the fried dough and pulled a chair back from the table for Croke. "I knows why you're here. There's only two things on your mind right now. When are we going for a poke and how fast do you think we will row?" Din laughed to kill himself.

"We can't practise all summer and not know how fast we could have gone," Croke said between swallows of touton.

"Don't worry, don't worry. I'd say we'll go next Friday or Saturday, if we gets a good pond. Even if there's a breeze, old Watt will ask us to be ready. He can estimate pretty close as to how much time even a small bit of wind will cost us."

Croke poured more molasses over his toutons. "There's iron in molasses, so they says. Glad I never bit down on a piece yet." He grinned. "Sometimes I wishes my backside was made of iron so I wouldn't get so many blisters on my arse." The grin changed to a grimace as Croke shifted in his chair.

"We needs to get a few more spins in the new boat before we rows for time," Din said. "You knows Watt decided that the last long row would be one week before the regatta. And whatever time we got left we'll need to practise starts and turning the buoys with the *Blue Peter*. She's some boat, ain't she? Cuts through the water like a blade. Never seen the likes of her. One thing for sure, I'd like to beat Torbay until they're black and blue. Them and that *Red Cross*. That boat don't have a patch on ours."

"McCarthy, you're crazy." Croke laughed. "That time they rowed in practice—what was it, nine twenty? That's pretty quick."

"I heard Watt say last practice that he thinks we're seven or eight seconds faster than what they rowed." Din wiped the molasses from his chin with one of Ellen's good napkins. She'd kill him, but he'd deal with that later.

"So you think next week we'll row for time?"

"Yes, b'y. Watt needs to know what we can do before Regatta Day."

They tied up at logy bay, the last long row over. "We'll row for time tomorrow evening," Watt said. "If it's windy, then Friday. If not Friday, then we'll try Saturday. We've had enough practice in the *Blue Peter*. You're a smooth crew and she's a keen boat."

Din felt like asking Watt a few questions, but he didn't. No one did, although he knew they were all thinking the same things. Did Watt think they were ready? If there was a wind, would they row anyway? How windy did it have to be to cancel the poke? Torbay had already set the mark. They'd shown Outer Cove what they could do, and now it was the cove's turn. Every man who held an oar during the final days of practice had a pit in his stomach. Not just the men of Outer Cove, but all the men in all the crews. You could almost smell the change in the air at the pond.

Chapter 23

Quidi Vidi could be breezy, loppy, or foggy at any time of the year, but during the final days leading up to the regatta, it was often beautifully calm. As the crew made their way to the boathouse, only the breaching brown trout broke the water's dead calm.

"Now, men," Watt began. He felt as if the pond behind him were waiting for the *Blue Peter* to come out onto it. The barns on the Ross farm were reflected in its clear mirror. He stood within a few feet of the crew. "There's only five times." He raised his hand, fingers spread wide. "Five times that you needs to listen to the times I will be calling out this evening. They're when you gets to the minute post, the gate to Woodley's house, the Virginia River, the turn, and the minute post coming back." Watt knew the men were nervous, except for John, who was as still as someone in a trance.

"What time do you want us at the turn?" asked Nugent.

"Torbay did it in four minutes, thirty seconds. We need to match that." Watt winked at him. "We aim to be faster."

During the final strokes of the warm-up, John spotted Dr. Rendell's chestnut mare and carriage under a tree on the Cottage Farm road. The two figures in the carriage were watching the crew approach the stakes. John quickly shifted his concentration back to the rowing.

Watt took out his stopwatch and let it run, stopped it, then rewound it. The crew went through their usual warm-up—ten minutes of light rowing—then they did a few practice starts at a race rate. The boat slowly drifted to the starting point. Watt reached down and grabbed the toggle rope. He choose stake two, buoy two. That's the lane he hoped to be in for the fishermen's race. The shell moved forward, the toggle rope stretching until it was tight to the stake.

"Are ye ready?" He checked his course bearing for the final time. "Go!"

The *Blue Peter* moved away swiftly, driven by a rapid sequence of seven quick strokes followed by seven slightly slower strokes of increasing length.

"Great start, men. Now, on two, keep it out long and push that water back toward me." The wake from Nugent and Boland's oars went by Watt like a small twister. The boat sat high on the water—it ran beautifully. "Fifty-eight seconds, minute post."

The shell cut through the pond, sending a gentle wake from its path to the shoreline. Watt knew the men were pushing their bodies to the limit, never surrendering to the pain creeping into their muscles.

"That's how we'll christen this boat, men. Every stroke gets the same pressure. Push those legs. Push those legs right at the catch."

The crew could feel the moist air run past their heads, giving them some slight relief as they grew hot, the blood rushing through their veins. John knew that in five minutes they'd be fighting real agony, and no cool breeze could soften that. As he led the crew at a relentless pace, he was grateful that his back had healed.

Watt called out, "Two minutes, seven, Woodley's Gate." He glanced down at his watch and then back up, waiting. "We're at the river. Three minutes, ten." The boat was running magnificently and the crew looked fresh. "We've got a fast boat." He would save his praise for the row back up the pond. "Thirty seconds and we're at the turn."

He slowly tugged the tiller ropes and the *Blue Peter* began the long arc of the advance toward the keg. Within seconds the buoy and the bow of the shell touched. "Hold water!" Denis and Martin lifted their oars clear of the buoy as it went by the side of the boat, the bow men—Nugent, Croke, and Dan—hauling hard to get the boat heading up the pond without losing too much speed.

"Four minutes, thirty," Watt yelled. "That's the time we wanted, men! Now, we need seven of your best strokes to get back up to speed. On the count of two, let's have them."

Lighting-quick catches grabbed the water, pushing it away from the boat. Watt started the seven count with vigour. "One, two, three . . ."

A cracking sound echoed across the water. The long shaft of Croke's oar rushed by Dan's blade. The *Blue Peter* drifted to a stop.

In his carriage under the tree, Dr. Rendell watched the boat suddenly slow down. "Pass me my glasses, Sexton. I can't see what the hell is going on." He put the opera glasses up to his eyes. "It looks like there are only five of them rowing." He picked up the reins, turned the carriage around, and headed back up the road, watching the crew dock the boat, get out of it, and walk to the boathouse.

"Maybe we should wait until they comes out of the boathouse before we goes over," Sexton said.

"No, I want to speak to them immediately. They had a good run going. I don't know what happened to number three, but he stopped rowing."

"Well, then let's go up to King's Bridge Road and take the long way back to the boathouse. Put those glasses down, sir, for the love of God, before we ends up out in the pond."

Dr. Rendell tied his horse to a fencepost at the rear of Mr. Summers' yard and he and Sexton went to the boathouse. Inside, Mr. Tilley, the caretaker, was examining the cracked shaft of an oar. Watt had told him that they were going to row the full course hard, and had asked if the *Blue Peter* was properly rigged and ready to go. Tilley had assured him it was. John looked at Croke, sensing that the man was proud of the strength he had displayed in breaking the oar, but he didn't want to show it.

"It broke at the oarlock," said Tilley. He passed the shaft to Sexton, who ran his hand carefully along its fine finish to the break in the wood. "It's plain to see why they stopped rowing," he said. "Where are the rest of the oars from the *Blue Peter*?"

"Over there." Tilley motioned to the open storage area.

Sexton picked up an oar and eyed it, put it down, and picked up another.

"These oars all seem alike," said Dr. Rendell.

"You're right. They are all alike, but they're not like the broken one. This oar don't belong to the *Blue Peter*." Sexton handed the shaft to the doctor. "See where it broke off? It's brownish, dark there. Someone changed the oar on number three. They put an older, damaged one in its place." Sexton turned to Tilley. "Do you let crews change oars around from boat to boat?"

"No, never. If an oar needs to be changed, I changes it."

"Well, someone changed the *Blue Peter*'s oar."

"Don't look at me, my son. I didn't change the damn oar!" Tilley turned and looked at the doctor and Sexton. "This place can get pretty busy this time of the year. There's only me here to handle everything. I can't watch everyone." He took a pouch of tobacco and papers from his pocket. When the cigarette was rolled, Dr. Rendell took out his pipe and struck a match for both of them.

"There were two crews on the pond besides Outer Cove just then," said Dr. Rendell.

Tilley puffed on his cigarette. "They were just a couple of crews from the Battery, young fellas. They wouldn't do anything like that. They hardly know how to row, much less mess around with oars."

"Someone switched the oar," said Sexton. "I put the new oars in the boat yesterday. You were here with Mr. Job when we done it. Who was the last crew to use the *Blue Peter* before us?"

Sexton, Rendell, and the Outer Cove crew followed Tilley as he wandered out through the door, took his half-smoked cigarette from his lips, and threw it in the pond. It hissed as it hit the dark water. "Torbay. Neddy used her last."

The late evening sun was fading over the Hanlon farm when Croke got home. "How did you make out with the row?" asked his father, Will. "You didn't tell us the crew was rowing for time when you left this evening." His tone was accusing.

"How did you know we rowed for time?" Croke stalled. He was tired and hungry and in no mood for his father's moods.

"Young Tommy Slater told me."

"No doubt!" Din shrugged his shoulders and threw his hat on a chair.

"Well, tell us, then. Did you row for time? Break a record?" said his mother, Catherine, as she placed a fork and knife next to his dinner.

"I busted my oar into pieces about six minutes into the row."

"That was unfortunate, my son. What will happen now?"

"Watt wants us to try again tomorrow or Saturday. We had a great run going, and an excellent turn."

"You must be some disappointed."

Din looked at his dinner, and then walked across the kitchen to the hall. He needed to wash, to change. Blood had soiled the rear of his pants. He hoped there was still some of that ointment left in the jar.

His sister Mary was coming down the stairs. She grinned at him. "Is it fun rowing with your buddies?"

Din bared his teeth at her. "Fun? Any man who would row for fun would go to hell for a pastime."

Chapter 24

Jack Nugent hadn't slept a wink. At least he didn't think he had. Between the wind and the steady pounding rain, and Mary up every two hours with the new baby, it had not been a restful night. When dawn broke, he was ready to get up. He was tired, but it was better to be doing something than lying awake in bed.

He could barely see the meadow through the rain-smeared window. What he did see, he didn't like. He put on his boots and strode out into the dim morning light, tripping against the dray and falling face first into the mud. He turned over and laughed. A rude way to meet the morning! He got to his feet and went to the meadow. The whole field of cut hay was drenched by the heavy rain. He looked at the fish flake. Thank God Mary had stacked and covered the fish last evening. Like most of the women, charged as they were with the work of the flakes, she had a fine nose for weather. He looked back at the meadow dolefully. He'd need more than prayers to save the wet mass in the field.

On his way back to the house, he stopped at the coop to collect some eggs. Watt kept telling them to eat as much as they could in the days leading up to the regatta. "Get lots of grub in you!" Well, Watt didn't need to tell him to eat. Eating was one of the best things in life, after all. The eggs would taste good along with a bit of bacon and some fish. His mouth started to water.

As he gathered the eggs, Jack thought about Victor, Dowden's boy. He had just died of meningitis. Victor and his mother had brought chicks to them last summer. Father Clarke, the old bastard, wouldn't let the Dowdens bury Victor in the cemetery in Torbay. The Dowdens were the only Protestant family in Logy Bay. "Those black Protestants," Father Clarke said. "Worse than lepers."

By noon, the wind was rising. Jack thought if he could just free the grass from the wet ground, it might have some hope of drying. There wasn't much hope that the crew would row today. He hitched his horse to the cart and set out to see the McCarthys.

"What do you make of the wind?" asked Jack. "Do you think we'll row this evening?"

Dan and Din looked at each other and laughed. They were out looking at their meadow, which was in the same shape as Jack's.

"There's always a big westerly blow after a good rain, you knows that," Dan yelled over the wind. "When it comes up like this, it can stay like it for days."

"Guess we'll see how things are in the morning." Jack got back on the cart. The wind gusted, whipping the stunted spruce along the road. They looked as though their roots were struggling to hang on to the rocky soil.

Saturday was windier than Friday. Huge whitecaps raced off shore, tumbling and breaking.

John woke to find the door to the barn loft had blown off its hinges. It lay broken in the yard.

"You're not going to try and fix that in this wind, are you?" asked Kate.

"I got bigger worries today than that broken door. We rowed six minutes on Thursday, we didn't row yesterday, and it don't look like we will row today."

"Sure, we lives in a windy country, John."

John looked out the window. Prince stood with his rear end to the wind. His long, black tail flicked around his flanks like a birch broom in the fits.

"I'm going to Watt's. If we can't row until Monday, we could be in a real mess." John left his meal of salt fish and brewis on the table and opened the porch door. A mighty gust blew into the kitchen, sending the framed picture of the Sacred Heart of Jesus over the daybed a-tilt.

When John arrived at Watt's, he was sitting on his front doorstep with his right arm resting on his knee and his hand tucked under his chin. His unlit pipe dangled from his mouth. His hair and shirt were fluttering in the wind.

"I didn't bother putting any tobacco in it. I can't light a damn match in this." Watt put his pipe in his pocket. "I know, John, I know. What's worse is that we can't row on Sunday, even if the weather improves."

"I don't like it," said John. "If we had finished our spin on Thursday, I wouldn't be so concerned. It's the uncertainty. I don't know how you feels. I think Mr. Mare would allow us to row on Sunday if the wind drops off. He was a rower, got rowing in his blood."

"He's the best president we've had in years. Not like some of them on the committee, who are only there because of their names. Some of them couldn't haul a clothesline, much less an oar." Watt spat on the ground.

"If Mare goes along with it, that's only half the problem solved," said John.

"What do you mean?"

"Watt, if we can't work at the hay on Sunday without permission from Father Clarke, we certainly can't row." John sat down on the step next to Watt.

"Father Clarke don't give a damn about us." Watt stood up. "Why would we need his blessing to go for a spin?"

"Watt, you knows people will start talking if we don't get permission from Father Clarke."

"Well, he's not going to like seeing my face at his door begging to go rowing on the pond. I haven't been to church for almost a year." Watt shook his head. "I can't see him letting us row on Sunday, John. It's not work in his eyes. Rowing don't put food on the table. And we're practising to beat the living daylights out of the crew from his parish."

"We've still got to ask him, Watt. Monday is the last spin before the races. If we don't row tomorrow, it means we've only rowed once in four days. For six minutes."

"Six minutes and ten seconds."

"If the wind drops in the morning, I'll head out to see Mr. Mare. I knows where he lives, on Winter Avenue. We got to try, Watt."

"If Mare says yes, who's going to Torbay to ask Father Clarke if we can row?"

"We'll all go. As a crew."

"Why do we put ourselves through all this? You'd think I'd have better sense after all these years." Watt tugged at the pipe in his pocket.

"Now, Watt, if you weren't at the rowing, you'd be bored to death. Say a prayer the wind dies overnight. I'll see you in the morning."

Watt grinned. "I'll ask Kitty to put the prayer beads on the clothesline."

Martin Boland looked out the open window of his tiny cottage on the Rocky Hills. It was Sunday morning. The wind had finally exhausted itself and the sun was shining on a dark blue sea. He was waiting anxiously for John to come back from visiting Mr. Mare. It was a perfect day for a row. He looked up the wooded laneway that led to the road for the tenth time. This time his anxious gaze was rewarded by the sight of Prince coming through the opening in the trees. John pulled to a stop beneath the window.

"Great news, Martin, they're putting the shells out for us. I wasn't the only one at Mr. Mare's this morning." John smiled. "If you're ready to go to Mass, then come on with me now."

"Just a minute, John. I got to get a few pennies for the poor box."

John looked at the shining sea while he waited, feeling the beauty of the day.

"How do you think Father Clarke will take to us asking to go rowing?" said Martin, climbing aboard John's carriage.

"If he don't drop dead of a heart attack when he sees Watt sitting in the pew this morning, we got some hope, please God." John flicked the reins. "We're going to get the McCarthys on the way. Nugent is getting Croke and Watt. Won't hurt to say a few prayers before we get there."

Mass was over. Watt took the lead up the lane toward the rectory, and the men followed quietly. He knocked on the door, hoping the housekeeper would answer. He felt like buying time. The curtain on the window of the door moved slightly. The door opened, but it wasn't the housekeeper. It was Father Clarke himself. "What can I do for you, Watt Power?" The expression on the priest's round face was guarded.

Watt cleared his throat. "Father, you knows with all the windy weather these past days we haven't been able to row—on the pond, that is. We couldn't practise for the races, and there's only a few days left."

"So, you are asking me for permission to row on Sunday, isn't that right, Mr. Power? Is that the one thing that brought you to church today?"

"If it wasn't for the windstorm, we wouldn't be bothering you." Watt moved back from the door.

"God created the wind, Mr. Power. Perhaps He is not a regatta supporter." Father Clarke permitted himself a smile.

"Yes, Father." Watt cleared his throat a second time. "We're here to ask you if we could work today. Work at the rowing."

"What good works have you done lately, Mr. Power? And why have you been absent from church? Do you covet rowing so much that you would come here and lie to me to fulfill your desires?" Father Clarke crossed his arms. He looked down at Watt on the doorstep. "You should not just avoid sin, but the occasion of sin."

Watt kept his feelings out of his voice. "I have my failings, Father, but I works hard and I helps my neighbours and I goes to church. But not to Holy Trinity."

"Is that right?" Father Clarke stroked the white collar under his chin. "You want to work at rowing on a Sunday?" He pursed his lips and stepped toward Watt. "Are your gardens kept, the hay cut and dried? Is your fish cured?"

"Yes, Father, yes." John spoke for them all. "We came here to see you with the best of intentions."

"Sure, we loves God's wind, Father. It dried me hay yesterday," Nugent joked. Dan jabbed him in the back.

"Father," Croke called out. "We are in good favour with our farms and the fish."

"Where did that young fella learn how to talk like that?" John whispered to Watt.

The priest stepped back into the doorway of his house. His face relaxed. "I give you my blessing to row on this holy day. You must kneel down now, and give thanks to the Lord for His blessings, including boats and ponds and strong backs."

The men knelt, and the priest prayed. Then they were back on their feet, heading toward the carriages.

"We weren't long going about it when Father Clarke asked us to say a prayer," said Din.

"Yes," said Jack. "The whole crew was on their knees quicker than a bunch of altar boys."

"I believes I have just witnessed a miracle," said Din to Dan.

Ponies hauling lumber and canvas milling around the shoreline and the sound of sledgehammers on posts echoing across the pond were the first signs of the transformation that would alter the banks of Quidi Vidi in anticipation of the thousands who would appear there on Wednesday, August 7. Watt watched the hustle and bustle for a moment and then turned to the crew. "Three days off don't mean nothing," he said, as they got ready for their second-last practice.

"It means my arse isn't as sore as it could be," said Dan. The rest of the crew laughed.

Watt sighed. Rowing for time today was out of the question.

Before they pushed off the wharf, Watt reminded them that the next time they rowed the full course at race pace would be in the fishermen's race on Regatta Day. "The pond is perfect for a poke, b'ys, but today we needs to prepare for Wednesday." His crew needed one more row to get the timing right. The endurance was there; they just had to make sure the balance was, too. Once they got their balance, the boat would gain speed from their strength. Two practices to go. Four days until the races. It was Sunday. Watt took off his hat and said a silent prayer that they would be in communion with the pond.

Chapter 25

Every window in the house was raised as high as possible to the breezeless air. The heat from the stove finally began to lessen. Kate put John's supper in the oven box, away from the flies that buzzed through the kitchen, ignoring the yellow flypaper hanging from the ceiling.

"Aunt Kate, can I go swimming?" asked Tommy, sticking his head in through the kitchen window.

"Swimming?" Kate ran the back of one hand across her forehead and shook her head.

"No, my son. You got work to do. Them hens can't feed themselves."

The boy's voice took on a pleading tone. "Sure, Walter Carroll and Walter O'Rourke are going. I won't be long, honest."

"I don't know, Tommy."

"It's so hot, and the river is nice and cool. Please? I'll be back real soon."

"'Real soon, is it? You better be home before dark or the mickaleens will get you. And them hens got to be fed first."

"I'll feed them, I will. And I'll get back before dark, I promise—and there's no such thing as mickaleens!"

"I want you home long before dark," Kate said, wishing John were back. "An hour before dark, to say the rosary."

The boys took every shortcut they could find to the swimming hole below Whelan's falls, running hard as if it were the first swim of the summer. They zigzagged across the newly cut meadows and jumped over every cock of hay in their path.

"Tommy, you told Mrs. Whelan you were going swimming," said John Fox. "Sure, you never swims. You always hangs around the riverbank."

"Well, I'm going in the falls today." Tommy raced ahead to avoid him. Would he really go in the water? There were butterflies in his stomach. He hung back.

"Do you have any money for the regatta?" Tommy asked Pat Hickey. Aunt Kate hadn't mentioned money to him yet. He knew they were going to see Uncle John row, but he didn't know anything else. He'd never been to the regatta before, but he knew there were good things to eat.

"Me mother said she'd give me five cents." Pat was chewing on a piece of grass and slapping the nippers away from his head. "I'll be buying some peppermint knobs as soon as I gets there."

Martin Roche ran up behind Tommy and Pat and burst between them. "You got to watch the men trying to walk the greasy pole out into the pond. You'll laugh till you cries."

"Me and Aunt Kate are going out in the morning, to see Uncle John beat Torbay. He's going to win the championship in the afternoon," said Tommy.

"I heard Torbay rowed a good time in practice." Dave Kinsella poked Tommy in the ribs.

Walter Carroll kicked tall weeds to the ground. "I don't believe it. My father says Outer Cove will win in that new boat, the *Red Peter*."

"It's the *Blue Peter*. Torbay is rowing in the *Red Cross*."

"There'll be hundreds and hundreds of people at the regatta," Walter said.

"Thousands and thousands, b'y. Sure, it's a big holiday in St. John's." Tommy looked for a spot from which to jump.

"What if it rains and they can't race?"

"Then they races on Thursday or Friday."

"How come you knows everything about the regatta, Tommy?"

"Uncle John is always talking about it."

They broke through the thick alder bushes and came out on the bank of the Big River. Soon their clothes and boots were lying in a heap beside it.

Tommy looked down at the swirling pool. His heart raced like the river. He wanted to jump, but his feet were rooted to the spot.

"You're only pretending to jump, Tommy. You're not going to do it."

"Quiet, Foxy. Leave him alone," Walter said.

"Don't listen to Foxy," said Pat Hickey. "He wasn't so brave the first time he jumped in, either. We'll jump in if you needs help, Tommy, b'y."

Tommy closed his eyes and blessed himself. The sharp granite rocks hurt his feet, but it took his mind off the water rushing by him. Suddenly he jumped off the bank, hitting the water with a splash. He felt his feet touch the bottom, and then he was back at the surface of the water with his friends' faces gazing down at him. Above their heads, the blazing sun reflected off the leaves of the birch trees, whose branches hung out over the river.

"You did it!" yelled Walter. "Kick your legs hard, now."

Thrashing madly, Tommy swam to the safety of the shallow end of the pool and grabbed a rock.

One by one, the boys jumped into the pool, splashing, laughing, and screaming. Their voices echoed down the valley. Hours later, under a fading sun, they tramped down the dusty Lower Road toward home, hanging on to each other like thistles to wool, stumbling along in their worn boots.

Walter O'Rourke turned off to cross the meadow to his house, giving Tommy a slap on the back before he left. "Now, b'y, you can go swimming with us all the time."

"I'm some tired," said Pat. "I'll probably fall asleep before we finish the rosary."

"Me, too," Tommy said. "I hope it's warm again tomorrow. As soon as I'm finished me work, I'm going swimming again."

John took prince's harness off, led him to the pound, and set him loose. He stood for a moment to view the blue haze over the thick woods above the Rocky Hills and the cliffs at Witty Cove, which were white with hundreds of seagulls that had begun their nightly roost. As he walked to the house, a snipe flew in the air above the bridge across the Big River. The whoop of its tail sounded in the evening air.

"We were waiting for you, John," said Kate, gathering up her rosary from the table. "My turn to lead this evening. How was your last practice?"

"Good. Rowed a bit longer than usual, but we had a good run going. After that long spell off last week, it was some good to be back at it." He slipped the suspenders off his shoulders and sat down. "Turned the buoy a couple of times, that was the only hard work. Where's Tommy?"

"Upstairs putting some dry clothes on. He went swimming with the lads and brought half the river home with him." She rolled her eyes. "I'll call him."

John rose and stretched his arms over his head. "I need a good night's rest, and I'd better get one tonight because you knows I'll hardly sleep tomorrow night. I never sleeps right the night before the races."

"Tommy, come down now," Kate called out. "Bring your beads with you."

Dan was struggling to print each word. He wanted the letters to be perfect. He checked the spelling over and over, guessing that certain words were right. Liz would understand, anyway. He thought about asking his mother to check the letter before he put it in the mail, then quickly decided against it.

"Dan, my son, are you almost finished? I'm going to have to fill the lamp again or you'll be in the dark." Ellen crept up behind him and pretended to look at the letter over his shoulder. "You should go to bed, b'y. You must be tired." She put her arms around him.

Dan placed his own arms over the paper. "No, Mother, I'm not tired. It's a long letter I'm writing. Liz needs to know my plans." Very soon he'd be sitting in another kitchen, far away from Outer Cove. What would he do in a new country? Sometime after his mother had left the room, he carefully folded the paper, placed the sheets in the envelope, licked his lips, pressed his wet mouth against the gum, and sealed the flap. He turned off the lantern and left the still kitchen. A sultry draft pushed its way through the open window at the end of the hall. The floor beneath his bare feet was cool and welcoming. He opened the door to his room, wishing Liz were there in his bed.

* * * * *

A whiff of pipe tobacco drifted past John as he rode the bucksaw through the dry spruce on the sawhorse. He didn't need to turn around to know who was standing behind him, leaning up against the side of the barn.

"Trying to keep your mind off it, John?" Watt walked slowly toward John. His mouthful of crooked teeth held the pipe in place.

"I suppose you're here so you can keep your mind off a few things, too?" John laid the saw aside, turned around, and went to meet Watt. "Come in for a cup of tea, b'y."

"Not today, John. I just came by to see how you are." Watt topped up his pipe and relit it. "You looks rested."

"I feels rested. I feels good." John walked along with Watt toward the house. "Sure you don't want to come in?"

"No, I'm heading home to cook. Kitty don't want me in the kitchen, but I needs to keep busy. I likes peeling spuds, there's no thought to it." Watt walked to the gate that opened to the road. "I'll see you around five o'clock. Come hungry." He laughed.

John smiled as he watched his friend walk off down the road. He and Kitty always put together a big feed for the crew on regatta eve. Kitty would leave as soon as they got there, not wanting to hear the rowing talk.

"What's that cooking?" asked Martin. "Don't smell like chicken, but it do, sort of."

"Did you slaughter a goat, Watt?" joked Denis. "It better be a big one. I'm gut-foundered."

Watt gestured at the two tables that had been placed end to end against the window that looked out on Kelly's Hill. "Now get yourselves a seat, and leave the one in the middle of the table for me." He opened the oven door to show off the large bird, roasted a golden brown.

"Jeez, Watt, b'y. Where did you get the turkey?" asked Croke.

"It come from the Lester farm, out in the Goulds. Dr. Rendell got her for us."

The crew gathered around the stove. "It must be fifteen, twenty pounds," said John.

"They're ugly when they're alive, but some nice when they're cooked," said Watt, taking the bird out and putting it on a platter. He began cutting the breast. Steam rose up and a rich aroma spread though the kitchen. "Sit down, now," said Watt. "We got a meal to eat and some talking to do."

Kitty came into the kitchen and served them, then left to go to her house next door. Watt was the last to sit down, carrying his plate with him.

"We'll say grace before we begin."

"I didn't think you'd be much for saying a blessing, Watt," said Din.

"This is no ordinary meal," Watt replied. He rose from his seat. "Before either of you lifts a fork, reflect for a moment on God and your families, and add a short prayer for a fine day tomorrow." The men blessed themselves and bowed their heads.

"Now," said Din, "can we start?"

"Yes, b'y, you can start. For the next half-hour, you don't have to take orders from me, because by the end of tomorrow, I promise, you're going to be tired of me bawling at you. Now, don't forget to leave room for the molasses pudding."

Watt sat back down and let them eat their fill of turkey before he broke into casual talk around the table. "Now, listen, b'ys. In the morning it will be the same as every regatta before. We goes to the pond as a crew," said Watt, pouring hot water into the teapot. "I'll take my carriage and get the McCarthys and Jack. John will pick up Croke and Martin."

"Where do we meet?" Croke had gotten up from the table and was following Watt around the kitchen.

"Both carriages will meet at Savage's Bridge. We'll take the road through the White Hills past the Cook farm, then go through the Gut. When we gets there, we'll put the horses in the meadow at Pittman's. We'll walk from there up to the boathouse, along the path behind Conway's. We'll need to limber up from the ride out from the cove. It's a nice brisk walk from the Pittman place—ten minutes or so, enough to get the blood pumping.

"I asked Tilley to keep an eye on the crews using the *Blue Peter* in the first races. Don't want that shell out of commission for repairs." Watt poured out the tea and passed around the pudding. "One more thing. We'll take to the water no later than ten minutes before the start of the race."

"Is that enough time?" asked Croke. "Which stake and buoy do we have?"

"Stake two, buoy two. Now, where was I?" Watt scratched his head. "Ten minutes is just enough time to break a sweat and get to the starting line." Watt clamped his hands on the back of his chair. "Enough time to feel the weight of the oar in your hands." He took his hands off the chair and laid them on the shoulders of the two men closest to him. "This crew is ready. You're in fine shape, the best I ever seen. We've healed our blisters and our backs.

"Neddy Gosse had better not be the one that changed the oar in the *Blue Peter* last week. If he did . . ." Watt took a junk of wood and tapped it slowly against the palm of his hand, each tap a little harder than the last. "If he did, and we can prove it, he'll wish he'd never done it."

The hinges on the porch door creaked. All eyes shifted toward it.

Kitty poked her head into the room, smiling. "You're still here. Some quiet, the lot of ye. Had enough of the rowing talk?"

"Yes, Kitty, we're just finishing up." Watt placed the junk back in the woodbox.

"I hope I can sleep, with all this in me gut." Martin rubbed his belly and rose up from his chair. "I haven't seen the likes of this since Easter."

The crew thanked Watt and Kitty, then walked out the door into a light shower of rain.

"Wind's from the south," said John, as he buttoned up his jacket and pulled his cap down over his eyes. "It's light—that's good. There's more warm weather coming."

They went out the Pine Line back to their homes. A gentle breeze pushed the soft rain into their faces. The cattle lying off in the distance on the Pine farm looked like carefully placed black and white boulders. The faint sun strained to break the low cloud cover. John parted with the rest of the crew at the top of Barnes Road, bidding them a good evening and a fine rest.

"Be ready at eight, Croke. Don't worry about a thing," said John. "You should sleep well with all that ballast in your stomach."

It was 890 steps from Outer Cove Road to John's gate. He liked to count them, the same way he counted the number of strokes it took to row the full course at Quidi Vidi Lake. If he made the walk to his house in the same number of steps, it meant his pacing was right.

"A little rain falling," said Kate as John walked into the house. "But I don't think it will last."

John pulled a chair away from the table and sat down next to his wife. "This will pass. Tomorrow will be a grand day. The crew is ready. We got two races, two chances to prove our salt." He took Kate's hand, feeling the warmth of their years together. "Where's Tommy?"

"He's tuckered out. All excited about going to the regatta tomorrow."

"Watt and Kitty cooked up some feed for us. I'm ready for bed, too."

"I was waiting for you to come home, my darling. I could use an early night myself. Tomorrow is going to be some day." Kate got up and held out her hand to him.

The low cloud made the evening slip quickly into darkness. The tide surged against the rocky cliffs, sending a rumbling sound through the cove. John's final thoughts as he drifted to sleep were about the precise placing of his hands on the oar, how his feet should be set in the footing of the shell. His knees would be bent slightly, to brace the load with the effort needed to move the boat out of the dead water at the start. He fell asleep curled up like a baby and woke in the same position.

Chapter 26

John pulled the brim of his hat down to keep the glare out of his eyes. The sun was skimming the stunted woods above Houston's on the Rocky Hills. As he and Prince passed O'Rourke's Lane, Croke's long frame, leaning against the trunk of a tree, came into view.

"You're right on time, John." Croke climbed aboard the carriage. "If it wasn't for Mother, I'd still be in bed."

"You had yourself a good sleep, I take it?" Prince lurched forward before John eased the tension on the reins. Croke jerked back in the seat.

"Jeez, John, your horse is some anxious to get out to the regatta." Croke laughed. "I'm not sure what was in that turkey, but I wasn't in bed five minutes before I was out like a cold junk. Sure, I believes I was in a turkey coma."

"You looks rested, Croke."

"Rested? I feels like I could row to Torbay! How about you? Are you ready?"

"I had a grand rest, didn't even wake up to have a leak."

The light breeze barely moved the sagging tops of the juniper trees that lined the Lower Road.

"Not much wind."

"Hardly any wind at all. Bit of an onshore breeze." John

shrugged his shoulders. "We'll battle a bit going down to the turn, I imagine. Tailwind might aid us coming back."

"There's Martin waiting at the end of MacDonald's Lane," said Croke. "He's pacing back and forth. Think he's anxious?"

"No, he's fine. He can't wait to get out on the pond, that's all. He loves the races, that man. Loves everything about them." John reined Prince in until he stopped.

"Morning, fellas." With a leap, Martin was up on the back seat. "Prince must know it's Regatta Day, the way he's trotting out the road."

"Wish he knew how we're going to do," said John, grinning.

"What do you make of the weather, John? Light wind, sunny." Martin leaned ahead and placed his hand on John's shoulder.

"I'm glad the races will go ahead. I hates delays. Can't see any records being broken with this wind, though. A southeast wind's a bugger of a wind, even if it is light. It acts like a damn tide when you're rowing into it." John pulled gently on the reins to ease Prince's pace. He didn't want to get to Quidi Vidi too early, only in enough time to deal with getting the boat set up.

"There's Watt, resting on the bridge. Having his last few draws of the pipe for the morning," said Croke.

"I doubt that," said John.

Martin looked at Croke. "You're excited, Croke, b'y, and nervous, too. It's a good thing we got a long ride to town before we rows. That'll give you a chance to settle down a bit. Don't get me wrong, when you're nervous, you're ready. And it don't hurt to hate the crowd you're rowing against, either."

"Morning, Watt," said john. "Let's get a move on." Watt climbed back up on his carriage, and the crew was off.

They crested the White Hills and rode along the edge of the tree-lined trail of the Cook property and the Waldgrove farm. Only tuckamore stood along the rock walls and fences that protected the crops from the cows in the adjacent fields. The lake was now in sight, its water blue and calm in the distance. As John got closer to the pond, he could feel his body relax.

The two carriages turned onto the north side road, slowing down just before the Gut. Out on the lake, four white, perfectly aligned kegs bobbed in the morning breeze. All seven heads turned to look at these buoys, which marked the turn.

It had been a short walk to their boathouse from Pittman's. Like a draft through an open door, the southeast breeze found its way up through the cliffs of Cuckold's Cove and pushed out onto the lake.

Watt led the crew through the crowds on the shoreline, giving them last-minute advice. "Going to have to take a wide sweep heading into the turn in this wind. Southeast wind can be tricky, especially if you gets a lead on a crew in the lane to your north side. That damn wind can take you over on the next buoy if you comes out too wide off the turn.

"John, it's nine forty. Let's you and me go check the race program, make sure what stake and buoy we're on. The rest of you, go into the boathouse."

John and Watt tracked down two programs. "John, my son, they must have made a mistake at the printers. Sure, there's no way we're on number four. They told me number two. I'm going to go find that Jesus Thompson and get this straightened out." Watt's search for the captain of the course proved fruitless. He saw Mare, the president, standing by the dock.

"Is this the final placing for the crews in the fishermen's race, sir?"

"I'm afraid it is, Mr. Power."

"Where's Mr. Thompson?"

"I'm not sure. Out there somewhere." Mare waved his hand in the general direction of the crowds, and turned away.

Watt went to search the boathouse for Thompson.

"Watt!"

Watt ignored John.

"Watt!" John caught up to him and grabbed his arm. "Even if we finds Thompson and curses him up in the clouds, he won't change nothing. We only got enough time to get the boat ready, warm up a bit, and head to the start."

"I'm about ready for a smoke and a drink right here and now." Watt finally stopped walking and looked at John. "You're right. Let's go get the crew and go to our boat. Maybe when I'm on the water I'll settle down."

"I'm sure you will, Watt, b'y. I'm sure you will."

As he asked the crew to push off, Watt saw the Kinsellas and Roches coming down Boathouse Lane out of the corner of his eye.

"Good thing they're on stake two and out of everyone's way," Dan whispered to John. "They never made it home last night, by the looks of them."

"Now, men, this is not a practice. No more talking!" Watt said. "Unless you got a question for me, there'll be no more words out of you." He stood up in the boat. "We got about six minutes to get to the start line. We'll row about three minutes, stop, and try a couple of starts. If the first start is good and we hit the rate we want, there won't be a second start." He sat down and tightened the tiller ropes. "Blades under the water.

Ready." The throng of people around the boathouse stared at them. "Go!"

The *Blue Peter* shot through the water as the rowers pushed her through the breeze that fanned out over the lake. The small lop breaking against the hull was no match for the six from Outer Cove.

"That's good, men. That's good rowing. Feel her break through the current." Watt counted the strokes in groups of seven. Seven catches, seven drives, seven finishes, seven recoveries. He liked that number. Five came too quickly and might make them rush the stroke. Ten was too long, especially late in a tight race. Ten could discourage a crew. To ask for multiples of ten hard strokes ran the risk of breaking a crew mentally. Seven was the perfect number. It never seemed like a number that couldn't be reached, even when the men were tired and suffering.

"Let her run. That was just under four minutes." Watt stood up for the last time before they went to the start line. "Now, let's get ready to try our start. We don't want to cool down too much. Bury those blades." He sat back down.

"Same start as always. One half-sweep, then a second half, three-quarters of a stroke, then a full sweep. Seven full strokes at full pressure. Stop after the seventh." Watt executed his commands with military precision. "Go!"

The crew's reaction was swift. They were like soldiers responding to a drill sergeant.

"We're up to speed on the sixth full stroke. No need to try another start." Watt took a deep breath. "Let's row to the start."

The early morning crowd was beginning to swell. The last of the tents were being raised. The crew's final practice strokes took them past the Marquee wharf. The band, led by Professor Power, tuned its horns on a bandstand decorated with bunting and the flags of Britain and Newfoundland, "the two Greatest Nations."

"When we gets close to the stakes in the start area, listen only to my voice," Watt said. The *Blue Peter* drifted along the shore, passing Gosse's crew on stake one.

Out of the corner of his eye, John looked across the small space of water that separated the two foes. He was quite certain Clements was looking his way, but he didn't want to look at the man. At the last minute, he locked eyes with Clements. The hatred was mutual.

"Move up, number three," called Thompson through the bullhorn. All four coxes held the toggle ropes, which were tied to stakes, taut. People on the shore stopped walking to watch.

"Are you ready, number one? Are you ready, number two? Are you ready, number three? Are you ready, number four? Are you all ready?" The committee boat had already rowed up to make sure the boats were in their proper places.

The gun fired and the flag dropped out of the president's hand. All four crews burst out of the start. The Kinsellas and the Roches jumped into an early lead in the *Daisy*. The light crosswind pushed the rippling waves against *Blue Peter*'s hull. Watt kept the tiller rope firm, making slight adjustments to keep the boat on course.

"One minute," Watt called to the crew. "We have a quarter length lead on Manning." He didn't tell them that Gosse's crew was less than a quarter length behind them. "It's early in the battle, men. All strokes must be hard. Full pressure on every single one—give it all you can. We'll see who falters first."

It was a three-boat race at Woodley's Gate. Watt knew Gosse's crew was fast, but where had this Manning crowd come from? There were two Torbay crews up against two

Outer Cove crews. He didn't give a damn. He'd have liked to be right between them.

Watt glanced at his watch as they began the approach to the turn. "Four minutes, twenty," he called. Manning's crew on stake three in the *Glance* was falling behind. Almost a boat length separated the lead crews and Manning. "We need extra effort here, men. We need to keep our boat speed. On the count of two, seven of your hardest."

Watt's back banged against the back of his seat. The gap between the *Blue Peter*, the *Red Cross*, and Manning's crew was widening. With four minutes gone, the *Daisy* was dead last.

"We still got a quarter boat length on Gosse. The lead is ours at the turn. Let's come away at the same." The rudder shot a rooster tail into the air as the boat rounded the buoy. But their lead was suddenly eclipsed by Gosse's sweep of the keg—there was a deadlock at the halfway point as the two crews came away from the turn.

"Watch out, John!" Nugent shouted. The bow of the *Glance*, two lengths behind, was just entering the turn, heading directly toward Watt and his crew.

"Stop rowing! Stop rowing!" Manning roared to his crew. "Hold water! Hold water!" he yelled, trying to slow his boat.

The *Glance*'s crew struck their oars against those of the *Blue Peter*. Watt reached out with his left hand and pushed the interfering boat away. Jack and Din began to row together with the bow-side oars. The cox of the *Blue Peter* wished he had longer arms so he could reach out and slug Manning.

"There's time enough left to make up this gap. We're clear of Manning's gang now. Pay attention." They were coming to the Virginia River, and Torbay had a lead on them of almost two boat lengths of open water.

"They're getting desperate. They can't hold that lead. Not like an Outer Cove crew can." Watt raised his voice like a colonel in battle. "Let's see if we can bring them back to us." The *Blue Peter* was riding a slight tailwind and advancing rapidly, but there was a little more than two minutes left to the finish as they swept past Woodley's Gate. One and one quarter lengths to make up, to salvage the race and season. Watt thought longingly of his pipe.

"Those long rows to Logy Bay are paying off. We're almost on their rudder." Watt knew the effort to chase and reel in Torbay was taking its toll on the crew. The whole year was on the line.

"You're fine rowers, men. Better than the best sailors in the Royal Navy." Watt had pushed them to within striking distance of the other boat. The nose of the *Blue Peter* was at the back of Gosse's seat. The crews stormed past the Marquee wharf—they were less than a minute from the finish line.

"They're fading fast," Watt said to John. "I'm at their rudder now." He turned to the rest of the crew. "On two, men, bring up the rate." They responded with vigour. John shortened the stroke and increased the rate for the final thirty seconds. He knew the count in the number of strokes remaining—eighteen to the finish.

Watt watched Gosse's crew speed up. They had doubtlessly heard him make the call to up the rate. "We're closing, John. Hold that rate. Hold it!" The crews collapsed as the gun fired to signal the end of the race. Some men fell on their oars, others onto the feet of the rower behind them. The shells drifted aimlessly toward the shoreline.

Dan leaned ahead and said to John, "I don't think we got the bastards." He pushed the words out between breaths. "I don't think we caught them. We ran out of water." He placed his hands on John's shoulders for a moment. Then his tired arms fell away.

Watt sat motionless. His eyes shifted to the right, where Torbay had begun to celebrate. Bright sunshine glanced off the still pond. Sweat flowed into his eyes. The breeze that had followed them up the pond had diminished. Inside Watt, a tempest was stirring.

"We're not staying for the results—we got second. Let's get out of here now." Watt's bitterness seeped through the six soaked bodies sitting in front of him. They took their oars and began the slow row away. "After we dock, go straight to the meadow behind Summers's and wait for me. I wants a meeting with Mr. Mare."

The words from the chief judge's bullhorn became lost in the noise of the pond-side crowd and the clomping of hooves on the approach to the boathouse. "First place, in the *Red Cross*, Torbay, in the time of nine thirty and four-fifths seconds. Second place, in the *Blue Peter*, Outer Cove, in the time of nine thirty-two. Third place, in the . . ."

People from Outer Cove waited on the dock with long faces. Watt nodded at them. The crew followed him to the back of the boathouse. "Stay here," he said to them. He went around the building and entered it. When he got to the president's office, he rapped on the door. Mare opened it.

"Good morning, sir." Watt reached out to shake the president's hand. "Mr. Mare, I would like a couple of minutes of your time."

"Certainly, Mr. Power. Come in. Have a seat. Close race out there this morning. What happened at the turn?" He sat down behind his desk. "I'd rather talk to the crews after a race than before one. You know how some people are."

"What I knows, Mr. Mare, are the rules of the pond. We had the lead and the right of way coming out of the turn. Pat Manning didn't give me the right of way. That's what happened. It cost us the race." Watt went to stand in front of the desk. "Now what chance have we got of rowing in the championship race?"

"I'm sorry, Mr. Power. Everyone makes mistakes. What can we do to Mr. Manning now, suspend him? His season is over. They came last."

"My crew should never have been on stake four. We were told we were going to be on stake two, right next to Neddy Gosse in the *Red Cross*. Manning's crew is young, inexperienced. They should have been on stake four, or somewhere out of my goddamn way. It's their first year in the fishermen's race. The Kinsellas and the Roches shouldn't been on stake two. Thompson got the Outer Cove crews mixed up. My crew should have been on stake two, buoy two. Didn't he know that Jim Roche and his crew are washed up? This captain, this Thompson chap, is an arse." Watt's face turned red. "Where'd he come from, anyway?"

"He's a cricket referee. A fine fellow."

"Cricket! Cricket! Mr. Mare, I wonders about your good sense, sir."

"Now, Mr. Power, I understand why you are upset, but insulting me isn't going to change the outcome of the race. The rules weren't followed. That's unfortunate. Manning should have stopped rowing, held water, but he didn't, at least not soon enough." Mare got up from his desk, went past Watt, and opened the door. "You've made your point, Mr. Power. I will ask the captain to investigate the incident and report to me."

"I hopes you're able to find him," Watt said. "You could

try one of them hop beer tents." He started to leave, then turned back. "Something odd is going on. Someone switched one of *Blue Peter*'s oars for a dirty old damaged one last week. And now this mess on the turn." Watt looked the president straight in the eyes. "I can't prove what's going on, but I knows something is. Good day to you, sir." He went through the door and slammed it behind him.

Watt stepped out of the boathouse. The wind had died down completely and the heat was intense. He went around to the back, where the crew sat in the shelter of a maple tree, passing around a bottle of water. He hoped it was water, anyway. Mike Snow was with them.

"Where did you watch the race from, Snowy?" asked Watt.

"Right at the turn. Looked like a set-up to me," he said, spitting on the ground. "Manning's crew is a bunch of youngsters. They shouldn't have been on stake three. I don't know why ye weren't on stake two."

"Come on, b'ys. Let's go back to Pittman's and get our carriages," said Watt.

"What then?" asked Martin.

"We'll go over to Ross's farm. Mr. Ross is expecting us."

Watt picked up his jacket from the ground and rustled through the pockets for his pipe. He looked at the crew. "When I sticks the tobacco in her, I'm going to pretend it's Manning's guts. Let's go. We'll head over to the farm, get a bit of grub in us, and try to figure this mess out." He tried his pockets again. "Damn it, I left the bloody pipe in the carriage."

Chapter 27

"Tommy, wake up!" Kate called up the stairs. "It's a grand fine day, there's sure to be a regatta, my son."

Tommy rolled over. The sun was streaming in through the window. He jumped out of bed, his hair tangled, his eyes half open, and ran down the stairs to the kitchen, his small, bare feet barely touching the treads.

Kate took one look at him and shook her head, smiling. "You go outside and use the toilet and then get back upstairs and have a wash, and I'll comb them knots out of your hair. And then come get your breakfast. And you got to polish your new boots, show them townie boys how it's done." Kate pulled the boy to her warm body and kissed the top of his head.

"I hope Uncle John won the race this morning," said Tommy. Then he squirmed away from her and ran out the door.

"They worked so hard all summer," Kate called after him. "If they loses to Torbay, it'll be the end of Watt Power." She turned away from the door and began to prepare breakfast.

Kate looked at Tommy and felt pride. He was dressed in a new white shirt and brown knee breeches with a jacket to match, and a cap that was a smaller version of the one John had worn out the door that morning. The boots glinted in the dim kitchen. She had sold enough fish in town over the summer to be able to afford to outfit him like a prince.

"We'll ride out to the races with Mrs. McCarthy. She got a friend on the Cove Road who'll keep her horse and carriage for her, and we'll walk from there to the pond."

"Do you think Outer Cove won the fishermen's race?" Tommy squinted as Kate produced a comb, wetted it, and started on his tangles.

"I don't know, darling. I don't know. Hard to say. Anything can happen with the rowing." She gave his hair a final comb-through and then fetched her new, wide-brimmed hat with the silk flowers. Taking him by the hand, she said, "We'll find out soon enough about the races, won't we."

"What in the name of God is that hanging off the cart up ahead?" Ellen looked at Kate, eyes wide, before turning back to the road. "Holy Mother of God! I believes that's Mike. Mike Kinsella."

She eased Belle to a stop. "I think he's dead. Hold on to Belle, Kate." Ellen got out of the carriage and headed for the cart coming toward them. She grabbed the pony's bridle. "Whoa there, girl."

The body of Mike Kinsella flopped over the side of the cart like a dead fish. His head was mere inches from the rocky road. Ellen reached down and tugged on his limp frame. His eyes suddenly popped open. They were bloodshot.

"What in hell's flames is going on?" He belched, and Ellen, wrinkling her nose, turned her head away from the smell of rum and vomit.

"Were you in the race this morning?" Kate called from the carriage.

Kinsella groaned. "Yes, Mrs. Whelan. We lost bad. Done for the day. So is Watt and his crew."

"What?" Tommy took his hat off, revealing a sweat-soaked head.

"He's been drinking, Tommy." Kate shook her head and patted the boy on the arm.

Ellen propped Kinsella up in the seat, complaining about the stink. "What do you mean, Watt's crew is done for the day?" She gave him a shake. "Are you drunk and lying? I knows you're drunk, that's for sure."

He licked his lips, leaned forward, and tried to focus. "Mrs. McCarthy, I swears to God Almighty, John, Dan, Din, and them lost the fishermen's race." Kinsella flopped back in the seat, spittle clinging to his beard. "They had a bad turn at the buoys. Hard luck. That's all I knows." The slurred words came out like eels moving through weeds in a creek.

"What else do you remember about the race, Mr. Kinsella?"

"That's all I knows, Mrs. Whelan. That's all." Kinsella, one eye closed, grabbed the reins and snapped them, drawling, "She's a smart pony. She knows her way home." The cart moved off.

"Oh my." Kate looked down at Ellen standing by the road.

Ellen jumped up on the carriage like a bird on the wing. "Let's get moving. I'm not saying Mike Kinsella is lying, but I knows what he said isn't the whole truth."

Kate nodded. "Let's go, maid."

Tommy held on to Kate's hand with the all the force he could muster. They had left Cottage Farm Road and stepped into the mass of people gathered by Quidi Vidi. His heart was beating rapidly and his stomach wasn't right. He thought that maybe he was really hungry.

"Where did all these people come from, Aunt Kate?" He gripped her hand even more tightly and huddled against her to protect himself from the bumping, rushing people milling in the afternoon heat. Kate smiled and waved at familiar faces.

The banks of Quidi Vidi had become a village of tents. The smell of meat stews, fish stews, Jiggs' dinner, hop beer, and sugary confections filled the air. Those drained of energy and money watched the newcomers arriving with excitement in their step.

Tommy's mouth filled with saliva. "Aunt Kate, I needs something to eat. I could take a bite out of the leg of the Lamb of God right now, I could. Sure, you must be hungry, too."

Kate dropped the boy's hand and turned him to face her. "I don't know where you got that kind of language, my son, but I never wants to hear it again. Do you understand?"

Tommy's eyes were stinging and his heart, which had settled down, was pounding again. He felt as if the sun had fallen out of the sky.

When she saw his face, tormented and white, Kate had all she could do not to comfort him. But profanity was a serious sin. Better his heart should suffer for a short time than his immortal soul forever. He was so young—them older boys, it was, leading him astray. She forgot her resolution and bent down and wiped Tommy's eyes. "Never mind, me darling. We'll go get ourselves a big feed and keep the Lamb of God safe this one day at least." The grin he gave her was better than the money in her pocket.

"Support the BIS orphanage," shouted a ticket seller. "Two cents a ticket for a chance to win this lovely prize. Just a few left holding up the wheel."

"Wait, Tommy. I wants to buy a ticket on that set of china teacups."

"Two tickets left on this exquisite prize," called the man, waving the final tickets in the air.

"I'll take the two of them." Kate raised her hand and passed him the coins.

Tommy peered at the pond whenever there was a gap between passing figures. A light breeze lapped the shoreline. Children rushed along, some with parents, some without. The gun fired, signalling the start or end of another race.

"Number thirteen is the winner."

Kate looked at her tickets and nearly lost her breath. "I have it! I have it!" she cried, waving the cardboard pieces. The teacups, with their purple violets and gilt rims, were hers. She'd have tea out of one of them that evening, see if she wouldn't.

"Thanks be to God, Aunt Kate, before I starves to death."

She tucked the cups under one arm and put the other around the boy. "Come on, young Thomas, let's go fill your belly."

Chapter 28

"Here comes Stephen Power up the lane. He got Mr. Savage with him. The old skipper wouldn't miss a regatta." Allan Ross was looking out the front window of his farmhouse. It was late afternoon, but the weather was still as pleasant as it had been in the morning. The shadows were a little longer, that was all.

"John Savage must be seventy-five," said Watt.

"More like eighty," Allan said, laughing. "They're coming by to get their horse and head home, I'd say."

"Not before they comes in and has a cup of tea." Agnes set out two more cups while her husband went to greet their new visitors.

"Come in, gentlemen, come in. You're not going to stay for the championship race?"

"No, b'y. Skipper's been here all day, and I got to get back at the hay," said Stephen. He looked around. The house seemed to be full of rowers. Watt Power and John Whelan at the kitchen table; Dan and Din McCarthy slumped on the daybed; Jack Nugent, Martin Boland, and Din Croke standing in a group, talking.

"Watt, did ye leave the pond right after the fishermen's race?" Stephen pulled up a chair next to Watt and John.

"As quick as we could get the hell out of there." Watt folded his arms across his chest.

"Well, I was there long after the race was over. All Torbay did was brag about their win. You should have seen them flashing those gold medals the governor gave them," Stephen said with a grimace. "What a goddamn racket. You almost caught them coming back the pond, and you near three full lengths behind at one point, thanks to Manning. He didn't have much to say to the *Evening Telegram* reporter when the fella asked what went wrong on the turn, the moron. I suppose there's not much chance of you getting in the championship race."

"Ours isn't a winning time." Watt turned his head to look out the window that had the pond in its frame. "As you knows, it's the two fastest winning times that makes the final. I just come back from the pond. I went over after all the races were done. The tradesmen got the second-fastest time, nine thirty-one and two-fifths. I had a word with Thompson and Mare. I told them that if the tradesmen don't show up for the championship race, we'll take their place. So we're waiting on whether the tradesmen will row or not." He dipped a spoon into his cold tea. "We'll know shortly whether or not we got to row again."

"Listen to me, now. Listen to me." Stephen placed one hand on John's arm and the other on Watt's. "I can't stay to watch the big race, but I hopes you row in it. Teach that Torbay crew, that Neddy Gosse and his bunch, a bit of humility."

The hands on the clock moved toward five. John had sat at the table all afternoon, watching the crowds through the open window. Roars rose up often, as the daring, and often drunk, fell into the water as another attempt to reach the end of the greasy pole ended in failure.

"I'm going over to see Thompson, to find out if he's had any word on the tradesmen," said Watt. "I suppose he knows the rules enough to know that if the tradesmen back out, we're the crew that takes their place. Come with me, John. Could take me an hour to find Thompson."

Watt and John left the house and began the short walk to the Marquee. Surely they would find Kelly there. Just before they came to their destination, they met Warren and Murphy from the tradesmen's crew staggering along the grassy slope.

"Hey there, Watt. Hey, old-timer!" barked Murphy, nearly falling against Watt.

"We got our win today, b'ys. You go get yours, now." Warren grinned and flashed his gold medal. Then he started to sing. "The tradesmen are winners, winners are we." He and Murphy clutched each other and stumbled past Watt and John, heading for the next tent that sold hop or spruce beer.

Watt and John hastened their steps. When they came to the Marquee, Mare and Thompson were there, as expected. Watt approached them and began speaking as soon as he had their attention, but Mare cut him short. "The tradesmen will not be contesting the championship. Be at the boathouse with your crew at seven. You will be on stake four, buoy four. Torbay has stake two, buoy two." Watt and John walked away from the Marquee in the direction of Ross's farm, each knowing the other was sorely tempted to break into a run.

"This is some crowd. Where are we going to, Aunt Kate?" She was practically dragging him along.

"To the boathouse, Tommy. I told Mrs. McCarthy I'd meet

her there. She wants to watch the last race, the championship race, with us."

"Will John and them be rowing in it? I heard some men talking back by that tent."

"It's all the rumour, Tommy, but I don't know. Dear Lord, I hope so." Kate tightened her grip on Tommy's hand as they bumped along between the hundreds upon hundreds of people on the shore near the penitentiary. "If they don't row again, it will be a disaster. Poor John will be in some hard shape."

"Disaster." Tommy looked up at her. "What's a disaster?"

"Oh, a shocking big mistake, Tommy. A big accident."

The late afternoon sun beat down on the trampled grass. Tommy and Kate shuffled along with the poor and the well-off, the sober and the drunk, the adults and children, the townies and the baymen. Smoke from wood fires billowed from the chimneys in the tents and the fires along the shore. The smell of cooked meat, onions, and fish mixed with the stink of sweat and alcohol.

The crew was growing impatient. Watt gently tapped his pipe on the stove and surveyed the room. "What are you going to do about this evening?" He pointed at Dan, but looked at Din. "This might be your last row with your brother, my son. The same flesh and blood in the same boat. What are you two going to do about Torbay?" Watt walked to the window that overlooked the pond and stared out. Then he turned around and fixed his gaze on Martin and Jack. "Martin and Jack, you makes the wash for the others to match. You're our strongest oars. What are you going to do about Torbay?" He looked at Croke. "Now, me lad." Watt placed his gnarled hands on Croke's shoulders. "You're going to try and break the oar, aren't you? That's what you're going to do about Torbay."

Watt walked to where John sat at the table. "I know what John's going to do." The sound of horse's hooves clopping slipped through the open window, breaking the tense silence. "John is going to lead you to the finish line and make sure you're there first. He's going to set a rate that no other boat can match, but you will be able to follow him." He placed his pipe in his pocket and looked at Croke. "Remember, keep your head in the boat. The race will be over before you knows it."

The walk from the farm ended at the steep downhill approach to the lake. Watt could see people from Outer Cove gathered at the dock, waiting for them. The crew went swiftly to where the *Blue Peter* was waiting for them. John straightened up his shoulders, remembering what Watt had said to them so often. "Always act like a king when you're at the pond. It don't matter if it's practice or a race, once that oar is in your hand, you make sure you knows who you are." The time for talk was over. There was no talking, even to the people who hung over the rail as he and the rest of the crew prepared the boat for her final battle of the day. Just as they were about to push off, the crowd along the rail parted for a man in a white dog collar. Father Clarke had arrived.

"Make way," cried Father Clarke. When he reached the two boats, he raised his right hand and carved the symbol of the Cross in the hazy summer air. The ruckus at the dockside stilled immediately. Some people knelt. "Bless these boats and the men in them, in the name of the Father, Son, and Holy Ghost. Amen," said the priest, and a murmur went through the crowd. The rowers stared at their oars for a moment, and then they pushed off. The crowd was suddenly boisterous again, cheering them on.

The evening was warm and cloudless. There was no

wind. The crews worked their way through the final warm-up, making the lake ripple. Watt watched Torbay row to the start as he gave his final instructions. Then the *Blue Peter* glided to stake number four over the quiet evening water, moving closer and closer to the thousands watching the two shells.

Croke glanced covertly at the masses. His family was gathered on the bank outside the penitentiary wall, shoulder to shoulder with the Flannigans, the Burkes, the Coadys, the Cadigans and many others who had come from Logy Bay. It was like a painting, and he was inside it. They all were.

The captain of the course gave his final instructions. John tried to spot Kate and Tommy on the crowded bank. He was sure he had heard the boy's voice. Then the starter's gun went off. All the birds near the water took flight in aimless panic. John's attention shifted again. Now the boat was his entire world.

Tommy looked down the pond through a slight gap between the people in front of him. He and Kate had fought their way close to the water, and although the two boats seemed large as life in the first moments of the race, they were small to him now. "Who's winning, Aunt Kate, who's winning?" He grabbed at her arm.

"I think Outer Cove has the lead," murmured a young gentleman peering through his spyglasses at the perfect catches of the six oars in the *Blue Peter*. They seemed like one set of blades chopping in and out of the water.

"You're wrong, buddy. Neddy Gosse's crew has the lead," said a swaying drunk, knocking the glasses from the man's hands. They fell to his chest dangling by the strap.

"Woodley's gate!" Watt roared. "We're neck and neck. Every man give me your best work, your best effort. Row the way a good soldier fights."

The crew pulled the *Blue Peter* through the calm lake at such a speed they could feel a draft of humid air whisk past their heads.

The roar of the crowd at the start of the race had turned into nervous chatter. Kate, Tommy, and Ellen watched as the boats approached the buoys. "Aunt Kate, Aunt Kate—sure, they looks just like them water beetles, don't they, like the water beetles in the Big River." Kate laughed and gave Tommy a poke in his ribs.

"Oh, me poor old heart. I can't tell who's first," said Ellen, her voice quivering. "Come on, boys, come on. Bring her around!"

The *Blue Peter* sped along, its wake pushing out toward the *Red Cross* on the stroke side and the shore on the bow. The seconds moved swiftly as the two crews charged down the pond. Except for his lips, Watt was as still as a wizard in a trance. "Now, men, we need more pressure." He saw the first signs of pain on their faces, but the boat continued to clip along. They rowed through the third minute.

Over the heads of the Torbay crew, John saw the tall marsh grass at the mouth of the Virginia River. The *Red Cross* wasn't giving an inch. The lead changed only when one crew finished a stroke and the other one began. There was a seesawing of small exchanges, Gosse pushing the six on the north side, Watt pushing back just as hard. The buoys were just seconds away.

"More legs on the drive, men." Watt hammered away at

his crew with every word he could think of—and some that seemed foreign to him. He knew the depth of their pain.

Reaching ahead to the catch, as if they were connected by one hinge, the six oars dived into the clear water like gannets. The crew pushed the footboards hard and pulled with their backs, each catch and drive made rhythmically and with full force. The *Red Cross* slipped slightly behind as the *Blue Peter* sped down the pond, its seven bodies animated by one soul.

"We're gaining. Great work!" Watt yelled. "Time to take the turn." The boats slowed slightly as they began the 300-foot arc. "Bring her in hard, b'ys." The *Blue Peter* cut across the wide arc around the keg. Nugent, Croke, and Dan quickened the stroke in rapid sequence. The stroke-side oars lightly shaved the swirling water, waiting for the call to join in. "Next stroke, Martin, now Denis, now John." At last, the *Blue Peter* had gained a slight advantage. "We got them by a quarter length," muttered Watt, as he eased the tension on the tiller ropes.

John and Martin were pushing torrents of water toward the stern of the shell. "We have them by three seats, John," Dan grunted. "The rate is spot on. Don't change it." John felt the hull of the shell slip over the dark surface of the lake. Every stroke was perfectly measured rhythm, power, and speed. The five behind him were keeping up.

"Let's have our first seven count," Watt called. "We'll open up some distance on Neddy's boys."

Their strokes like a flurry of punches from a heavyweight boxer, the crew forced the *Blue Peter* up to full speed. The wake from its hull streamed out, entering the water around the *Red Cross*, which was slipping farther behind.

"Virginia River," Watt hollered. "We got half a length on 'em. Me back's snapping against the board. Ye are starting to knock them down, but not enough. On two, let's push those legs, right from the catch, full pressure for seven."

Jack and Martin continued to drive the water off their blades, turning the near-black water into white whirlpools.

* * * * *

"Oh, Tommy, I think Outer Cove has the lead. Martin Boland seems closer than Tom Clements," said Kate, biting a fingernail. "Dear God, come on, John, come on. Row harder, row!"

"I can't see!" Tommy wailed.

"Do you want to see the race? I'll raise you up, young fella," said the drunk. He reached for Tommy, but staggered back and fell into the pond. There was a burst of laughter from the crowd.

"Here," said the man with the spyglasses. "Take these, and I'll put you up on my shoulders."

"Mary have mercy on us, I believes they are in the lead," shouted Ellen. "Come on Dan, come on, Din!"

Mary Nugent wedged herself in next to Ellen and Kate.

Tommy got down from the man's shoulders so that he could jump up and down, which he did, over and over. "Uncle John's going to win! He's in the lead! Holy jumpin's!"

"Woodley's Gate, men, two minutes to go. We got three quarters of a length. Hold that pressure! Hold it!" Watt yelled.

The *Blue Peter* pushed on. John's stroke was perfect. He felt like a clockwork man, as though someone had wound him up and he had no choice but to row half a second for the sweep, two thirds of a second for the recovery. He counted to himself over and over: one on the drive, one thousand on the recovery.

"We got open water. We got open water. God bless ye, b'ys," called Watt. "Less than a minute left. Thirty-five strokes to the finish. On two, John, bring up the rate."

John didn't have to be told to bring up the rate. He knew Watt wanted the crew to row those last seconds as hard and fast as they could. Even now, each blade followed John's stroke exactly, the crew's catches slicing the water in quick succession, the shell still perfectly balanced after nine minutes of war.

The gun fired to mark the end of the race. Outer Cove shot across the finish, the winners. The whole crew collapsed back onto each other with their final stroke. Neddy Gosse yelled and yelled, but his crew could give no more. Torbay, now three lengths back, gave what little they had left in defeat.

The crowd on the dock was in a frenzy, sensing that the record for time had been broken by the *Blue Peter* in her maiden championship race.

"They done it, Aunt Kate!" Tommy suddenly felt the boiled dinner he had consumed heave in his stomach. He pushed through the human barrier in front of him until he was in front of the water. As he bent over, he felt a cool hand pull the hair away from his face.

The Crokes, Bolands, and Nugents, standing beside the prison wall, watched the fury and speed with which their sons crossed the line. They cheered and hugged each other like excited children. The shallow water along the shoreline at the end of the lake was suddenly filled with dozens of people. Watt's neighbours, the Malones, Ryans, and Kellys, plus many faces he couldn't place, were there. Mike Snow, the Rings, and the Mallards jumped into the pond, splashing water over the victors.

The crew in the Torbay shell were motionless, their heads bowed.

Watt leaned ahead and grabbed John. "We done it, Whelan! You set the rate, and we done it. God love you, John. God love you."

The *Blue Peter* had come to rest a few feet from the shore. Kate and Ellen were there, waving, smiling, and blowing kisses. Tommy was jumping up and down, yelling, "Uncle John! Uncle John!" John heard him, and waved.

"Do you think they broke the record?" asked Ellen.

"I don't know, my dear," said Kate. "I'm some glad they won, though. There'd be no living with John if they'd lost. But look, that man is putting a bullhorn up to his mouth."

Mare stood on the judge's platform. He waited for the crowd to calm down before he spoke. "Ladies and gentlemen, here are the official results of the championship race." The crowd grew silent. "In second place, Torbay, in the time of nine minutes and twenty-one seconds." There was a short burst of applause. "In first place—and the 1901 St. John's Regatta champions—Outer Cove, who have set a new course record of nine minutes, thirteen and four-fifths of a second."

Hats of all kinds flew into the air, and people danced jigs. The crew raised their hands above their heads and then slapped one another on the back. Martin and Jack stood up in the rocking shell, shook hands, and then embraced. Croke looked at the faces staring at him. It was like a dream, but, for the rest of his life, this day on Quidi Vidi would be more real to him than many of his days.

"Let's go for a victory row and show our thanks to the crowd." Watt gripped the tiller ropes. "I'd best stand up and tip my hat to all those people on the bank." The *Blue Peter* circled the judge's platform.

The chant started with just a few voices, but within seconds a chorus of "nine thirteen, nine thirteen, nine thirteen" thundered across the pond. The clapping and cheering followed the crew back to the dock, where hands reached down to help the crew up. They tried to make their way through the mob, but to no avail. People would not let them by without shaking their hands. "We won't get out of here tonight," Martin whispered in Jack's ear. "Sure, these people are all gone mad!"

"Mr. Power! Mr. Power!" shouted an *Evening Telegram* reporter. "How do you feel about breaking the record you set in the *Myrtle*?"

"It's like this, b'y. I was with six great men back then, and I got six great men today."

"I got an idea," said Jack. He motioned to the crew to grab Watt. They lifted him up on their shoulders, which seemed to help their progress. Watt was raised high above all the others in the beauty of their victory as the sun sank over Mount Carmel Cemetery. Sunk, too, were the hopes of the Torbay crew, who slowly moved to shake hands with the victors.

Chapter 29

Croke handed Watt the bottle of rum. The cox drained the last ounce. The seven men climbed out of the carriages and stumbled into the dim evening light of Pat Fox's yard on the Rocky Hills. The commotion from the open windows spewed down to the river valley below. A steady roar of voices, mixed in with fiddle tunes, greeted Watt and his crew as they entered the narrow porch that led to the kitchen.

Tommy came running and wrapped himself around John. John looked down at him.

"Where's Aunt Kate?"

"Oh, she's here somewheres. I'll go get her." He rushed off, poking his way through the crowd.

"Look who's here!" shouted Kitty Fox, running at Watt, her arms open. She squeezed him hard. "By God, we'll wallop her down tonight, b'ys." Kitty grabbed Watt by the arm and jigged him across the kitchen floor. The rest of the crew weaved their way across the crowded room.

"Move aside, folks. I got a keg here just for the champions," hollered Pat Fox. "I'm the bartender," he said, laughing. "The rest of you better stay clear of it."

Croke took a jug of the brew from Pat, placed it to his lips, and downed it in one swift guzzle. He felt a warm, soft touch at his arm. Someone had managed to reach him through the swarm of bodies. He turned and looked into the blue eyes of Mary Carew.

"You rowed a great race today, Din." She pulled on his arm, seeking to get closer. "They said you couldn't replace Jack in the boat, but you done it. You won." She pressed herself to his side. "This is from the whole cove." She smiled, tilted her face up to his, and kissed him. Her lips and the skin of her face were so soft. He felt embarrassed for his day-old growth of beard, and was glad their embrace went unnoticed by the raucous crowd. His knees turned from wobbly to weak. His heart racing, he reached down, took Mary's hand, and led her to the door. They slipped outside into the cool of the August night.

"Let's hear it for the crew," said Pat Fox, standing on the woodbox. He had to yell to get the attention of the revellers. "To seven wonderful men, who were a real credit to the cove today." Barely penetrating the wall of noise, he raised his glass and shouted more loudly. "Three cheers for Outer Cove!" The crowd raised their drinks high. "Here's to all your hard work, and especially yours, Watt. The best skipper on Quidi Vidi!"

The evening light vanished and the first stars popped into the night sky. Lanterns shone through the windows of the Fox house like beacons for the dark cove. Fox's open door continued to welcome a steady stream of visitors.

"Tell us, Uncle John, tell us again," said Tommy, sitting on the floor in front of the mob gathered around John. "Tell us when you knew you was going to win the race."

John could feel the room sway. The heat rose up to his head. "I never seen the likes of the wash coming from Martin and Jack's blades, and Croke's, too, as we passed the Virginia

River coming back up the pond. It was then I upped the . . ."

He felt a slap on his back and saw a hand with a jug of beer in front of his face. He grinned. "B'ys, slow down with the beer or I'll never get through the night. Where was I? Well, we were coming off the turn and I looked over my left shoulder and Torbay hadn't quite rounded the keg. It was then I knew we could have the win."

"I thought you was cracked when you asked us to row to Logy Bay," Jack Nugent said, patting Watt on the back. "But that's where we had it over Neddy's crew. Their boat slowed down in the second half of the race, and ours never."

"You hit the nail right on the head, Martin." Watt laughed. "We were in better shape than Torbay. Well, when I sees Dr. Rendell again, I'm going tell him that what he told John was true."

Dan felt a warmth at his side and thought of Liz. He turned his head to find stout Maggie Carrigan curled up around him. Her dress and most of her petticoat were off. He suddenly became aware of something pricking his skin in the places Maggie wasn't touching. It took him a moment to realize it was hay. He wondered whose loft he was in, but then Maggie's heat and his tired body and the fumes in his head took him back to sleep.

Morning dawned over the rocky hills, guiding the last of the revellers back to their houses, back to their sleeping families and farms. Songbirds chirped their waking calls at the exhausted few traipsing the rocky roads.

Martin lifted the porch door latch and entered the kitchen. He jumped, startled by the figure on the daybed snoring like a bear. Then he recovered himself and had a look. It was Dan McCarthy. He shook him, saying, "Dan, Dan."

Dan sat up. He moaned and held his head in his hands the way Father Clarke held the chalice at Sunday Mass.

"What are you doing here? Last time I seen you, you were with Maggie Carrigan."

"Oh God, Martin, don't remind me," said Dan, squinting his eyes. The morning light was like a knife in his head. "The Lord have mercy. I'll never take another drop. She's a lovely woman, all the same, poor Maggie. Although I thought I might have had two women there when I put me arms around her." Dan burst out laughing, and then groaned.

"They don't call her the *Great Eastern* for nothing," Martin said, grinning. "Anyways, b'y, I'm going to bed. Haven't slept yet."

An easterly breeze crept in through an open kitchen window and down over Dan huddled beneath the quilts. He tried to drift off, his hazy thoughts travelling between memories of the race and the time at Fox's and his hangover. The Sussex clock on the oven box ticked away, harassing his headache. It was time to go home.

"Din, Dan, are you going to stay in the bed all day?" Ellen banged the door shut as she walked into the kitchen. "What time did ye get home, or don't ye remember?"

"Daylight, mother, daylight," mumbled Din through a crack in the bedroom door.

"It's two o'clock in the afternoon. You must have all that drink slept off by now." She poked her head into Dan's room. "My God, this place smells like a tavern."

"Then open the window, Mother. The Pines are spreading manure today. You might like that smell better."

"None of your sauce, Dan," snapped Ellen. "I spent most

of the morning getting together things to put in your chest. Boston isn't that far off for you."

Dan rolled over. "I'll get up in a few minutes. Put the kettle on, Mother, for the love of God."

"Yes, my son." She leaned over and kissed him on the head. "I'll gladly get you a cup of tea. But after you finishes breakfast, I wants you to head straight to the Big River and have yourself a wash." She rapped on Din's door on her way to the kitchen. "Get up now, Din. I suppose you'll have some tea, too?"

"Yes, Mother, I'll have a cup. Make it good and strong," Din growled. "Like the bark."

The punts tugged on the ropes that held them to the grapnels on the sea bottom of the cove. A light breeze gently moved them from side to side within the quadrant ruled by the swirling winds that criss-crossed the water. The fish had moved off shore, but the marker buoys for the traps still dotted the coastline to Torbay Point. Soon, the traps would be taken in, marking the close of the fleeting summer. The men and women of the cove, who had toiled so hard during the hectic fishing season, would finally have a rest.

"Kate," said John. "Are you coming with me to the McCarthys'?"

"I seen Dan after Mass on Sunday. I can't bear another goodbye." Kate looked at John and then at Tommy, who sat quietly eating a slice of gingerbread.

"I'll be back in an hour or so." John took his cap off the wall hook. "Then again, I might be less than an hour. Don't want to poke my nose into their last few hours."

"It must be hard on a mother," said Kate, "a son leaving home."

"At least Din will stay in the cove." John put on his coat.

Din caught Belle and led her to the barn. He could see Ellen at the kitchen window, Dan beside her.

Dan's eyes shifted to the yard, then back to his mother. Each sight of her weighed on him. He was trying to find the right words to say to her, words that would say he was both sorry and glad to go.

"The mare is tackled up," said Din from the doorway.

Dan stepped close to Ellen as she rose from the chair. His eyes filled, and the tears flowed down his face. He embraced her, his powerful arms meeting around her small back. He touched and then kissed her hair. There was some silver in it now. "Goodbye, Mother. I'll come back home again someday."

"I knows I'll see you again, Dan. You and Liz and your youngsters. Don't take too long about coming back, my son. You're young and you have all the time in the world waiting for you, but I don't. Liz will be some happy when you lands there." Her voice was muffled by his shirt.

"I suppose she'll be." He cracked a grin.

Anxious to get moving, Belle tilted her head and nickered. Din helped his brother lift the chest aboard the carriage.

Dan couldn't look at his mother, standing there alone in the doorway. When he was in the carriage, he turned and waved to her before it disappeared into the thick stand of spruce lining the narrow laneway. Except for the noise of the carriage wheels on the rocky road, the long ride to town was silent. The hurt in the brothers' hearts lay in the stillness between them.

"You'll look after mother, won't you?" said Dan. They had arrived at the harbour. Dan was contemplating the ship at anchor, which would take him away from all he had ever known.

"Of course, b'y. I'm not going nowhere." Din looked up at the plumes of smoke rising from the *Dartmouth*'s stacks. "Do you think you'll row in Boston? You know, in a regatta."

"Row in Boston? Sure, I don't know . . . I doubt I'll be rowing in punts if I does row." Dan inhaled deeply, looked down, and kicked a pebble out into the ocean. He shook his head to try to stem the oncoming rush of tears to his red eyes. "How did this happen, me leaving home?" He picked up his bag. "I don't know if I even wants to leave."

"Liz is waiting for you." Din reached out to shake his brother's hand for the last time. Dan's grip on his hand was like a vise. "Those big mitts of yours. Watt knew who to put on number five oar. We'll never replace you in the boat."

"Well, b'y, this is it. I'm off to a new land." Dan stepped on the gangway with his heart on his sleeve.

"You can always come home," Din shouted to him as walked aboard the ship.

Dan looked at the old city from the deck of the *Dartmouth*. Breathing in its salty, smoky air for the last time, he watched horses and ponies shuttle to and from the busy docks. It was easy to spot the big dappled grey mare as she rounded the corner and moved out of sight.

He was sitting on the bed in his stateroom, thinking about going to find the dining room, when there was a light tap on the door. Before he could get up and answer the knock, a porter opened the door and poked his head in.

"Mr. McCarthy, would you mind terribly moving to another cabin? You were allocated this one by mistake. It's not for a single person, but a family. We'll move you to first-class, if you're agreeable." A young woman squeezed her way past the porter into the room. She looked at Dan imploringly. He glanced out into the corridor and saw a man and two young children. Her husband, no doubt, and youngsters.

"Yes, sir, I'll shift myself directly." Dan got up and followed the porter down the hall and up a stairway.

"Thank you for accommodating the Mullins family, Mr. McCarthy. Seems there was a mix-up in the bookings. I'm sure you'll enjoy your stay in first-class. We'll have your trunk sent up immediately." The porter placed Dan's bag inside the door of his new stateroom. "Have a pleasant voyage."

When the ship sailed, Dan sat beside a portside window, watching Signal Hill. The signal pole was flying three flags: Murray's, Steers, and Baine Johnston. The ship pitched and rolled with the tide, making a wide arc as it left the Narrows and headed for the open water. Dan placed his face close to the porthole and watched the Narrows become smaller and smaller. He decided that the ache in his belly was hunger, not homesickness, and went to find the first-class dining room. It turned out to be a large room, gleaming with white tablecloths, napkins, china, and silver cutlery. He had never seen anything like it before. It made him feel shy and about a foot smaller. Just before he turned to leave, he caught sight of a man nodding at him and beckoning to an empty seat at his table for two. Dan was about to shake his head and turn on his heel, when his bellyache got the better of him. He walked to the table and sat down. He'd figure out what to do with all the fancy trimmings later.

The man stood up and extended his hand, and Dan shook it, noting his new acquaintance's expensive suit and fine leather shoes. A book, *Great Sailing Voyages*, lay face down on the table. They sat down, and Dan placed a linen napkin on his lap. He had seen the man remove one from his lap when he stood up.

"Sailing for Halifax or Boston? I'm heading to Boston to visit friends," said the man in a pleasant voice. His accent was that of the rich.

Dan felt a stab of unease and looked down at the table. "Boston."

"You have a girl there?" The man's voice was warm and friendly. Dan felt his unease subside. He looked up.

"Yes, sir, I do indeed have a girl in Boston. Her name is Elizabeth Malone, and we're getting married as soon as I gets there. Well, not the very moment. You knows how long it takes women to get ready for a wedding." Dan grinned. He felt nothing but hunger now. "My name is Dan McCarthy. I'm from Outer Cove."

The man grinned back at him. "I know you. You're one of the McCarthy brothers who rowed the regatta course record in the *Blue Peter* this year." He leaned forward, his eyes shining. "That was the greatest row I've ever seen on the lake. That record will last a long time. Watt Power and your crew are gifted rowers."

"You seems to know a lot about rowing, sir."

"I'm sorry, I forgot to introduce myself. I'm Dr. Rendell. Dr. Herbert Rendell. I designed the *Blue Peter*."

"You're the man who designed the *Blue Peter*?" Dan almost stuttered the words.

"Bob Sexton built her, as you know. He's a remarkable craftsman."

"That he is, sir, that he is."

The doctor looked through a window at the cliffs of Signal Hill. "I saw you study those flags on Signal Hill as we left the harbour. I guess you won't be going to the seal hunt next spring."

"No, sir. Me and me brother Din was there last spring. Hard work, it is." Realizing that no one in the room was wearing a hat, Dan took his off and hung it on the chair. His coal-black hair contrasted well with his neatly ironed white shirt. "We were meant to go on the *Southern Cross*, but by some stroke of luck we ended up on a Bowring ship instead, the *Aurora*. I mean, we never wanted to go on a Baine Johnston ship because . . ." Dan came to a halt, embarrassment and confusion preventing him from continuing. Sure, this man wasn't interested in any of that.

"It wasn't such a stroke of luck. More like a stroke in time." The doctor crossed his legs and placed his hand under his chin. "John Whelan told me that if you and your brother were to take a berth with Baine Johnston, that would be the end of the crew that he and Mr. Power were trying to build."

"Well, sir. Did he, now?" asked a bewildered Dan. He tried to imagine John Whelan in conversation with Dr. Rendell, and failed. That John was a deep one.

"I know the owners of the *Southern Cross* well. Let's just say they owed me a favour."

"So it was you who had me and Din switched to the *Aurora*?" Dan's expression was a combination of disbelief and dismay. What did this man think of him and Din?

"Yes, it was I. Don't get me wrong, Mr. McCarthy. I fully understand why you and your brother were forced into making such a painful decision, and I was happy to be of assistance in delivering you from it." He smiled and patted Dan's hand.

"Now, I think it's time we caught that waiter's eye and had ourselves a glass of whisky, don't you?"

Chapter 30

"John, I think you're going to have to keep your promise to Tommy today," said Kate, looking out the window as Tommy rounded the corner at Barnes Road in full flight. "Your promise to take him out in the punt. That's if he don't tumble and hurt himself before he gets to the door."

"I'll take him out for a spin around the cove." John rose from the daybed and stretched his arms over his head. "We won't be long. I'm still sore from digging all them potatoes yesterday." He walked up behind her and wrapped his arms around her firm waist. "Thirty-seven and solid as a rock, my dear," he whispered in her ear. "I can still work with the best and row with the youngest."

The porch door flew open, banging against a bucket.

"Let's go rowing, Uncle John," said Tommy, his chest heaving. "The ocean is flat calm."

Kate slipped out of John's arms. "Get your school clothes off now, Tommy, so you can go down to the beach with Uncle John." She took his books from him and placed them on the table.

The beach rocks crunched beneath their boots as they pushed the punt down to the landwash. The weak tide barely generated enough swell for the boat to catch a lift at the launch.

"We got to push as hard as we can to get her in the water," said John.

Tommy grunted and heaved, and together they moved the punt away from the rocks until its bottom rested partly on the ocean.

"You get in and I'll shove her off." John held on to the boat while Tommy climbed aboard. He sent the boat out into the sea, quickly jumping over the side before it had gone too far, and sat down beside Tommy. He took an oar, slid it into the thole-pin, and placed the end in Tommy's hand. The boy's hand barely fit over it. "Here you go, now. I'll grab the other one." The boat slowly drifted away on the open water.

"Tommy, where you're a boy, you have to use both hands on the oar."

Tommy looked up at the cliffs and chopped his blade into the still ocean. "I don't mind. Sure, that's the way ye does it when ye races, one oar to each man."

John smiled at him. "That's right, my son. Now, the next time you drops your blade in the water, pull the oar toward yourself, and I'll do the same. You're the stroke oar, and I'll follow you. That's grand, Tommy. You knows what to do."

"I think I learned from watching them rowing out the harbour all the time. I always pays particular attention to the way Martin and Jack rows together," said Tommy, making short strokes. He looked down into the dark sea, then back up, watching the beach move farther and farther away from him as the punt went past Witty Cove. Small whirlpools formed in the water as the blades pushed the boat along. Along the bottom of the rocky cliffs, seaweed floated on the top of the water, soon to be submerged by the approaching evening tide. Stroking evenly, side by side, the pair in the punt were soon far from shore.

"We'll have a rest, now, Tommy, my son. We come a good ways for your first row."

They put their oars across the gunwales and rested. A gentle swell rolled beneath them. Looking back at the cove, they saw a lone figure sitting on the grassy bank.

"You can't be out on the water for long before someone is watching you," said John. "I suppose that's a good thing, too. If we tipped over, he'd let the rest of them know. And then we'd be saved."

"Why do you think he's there, Uncle John? Sure, it's only you and me on the water."

"Some people don't rest easy, Tommy. I mean, some people's minds are always at work." John placed his hand on Tommy's shoulder. "He never does stop coming to the cove and watching us all row out to sea. He can't stop, my son."

"Do you think you can stop, Uncle John? I mean, do you want to stop rowing?"

John looked down at his weathered hands, inches from Tommy's small fingers. The boat had barely moved since they'd rested their oars. "I don't know."

"Do you suppose Watt is watching me row?"

"There's no doubt he is."

"Will I ever be as good as you, Uncle John? Do you think I could row faster than nine thirteen?"

"You mean nine thirteen and four-fifths." John put an arm around Tommy and squeezed him gently. "Maybe, if you works at it. It takes a lot of practice, a lot of work to set a record, and even more to break one. You needs good men in the boat with you. Men you can depend on, and a coxswain you can trust."

They slid their oars into the water and started toward shore. Tommy gritted his teeth and pulled with all the strength his small arms could give the oar. The punt glided over the calm ocean. Herring gulls moved overhead, sounding as if they were in pain. A slight change in the tide helped the boat along. Out at the horizon, there was a hint of blue sky.

"Your first row was very good," said John, as the punt butted into the sandy gravel of the beach.

"It was calm today, Uncle John, calmer than the pond."

They pulled the punt up on the beach, away from the rising tide. A hint of tobacco smoke drifted by them as they turned toward the bridge. The grassy bank was empty.

John gathered the stiff salt fish from the tinder-dry flakes. He pulled the brim of his hat down to shade his eyes from the descending sun and then finished placing the final catch of the season, now ready for market, in waist-high piles.

As he worked, he wondered, as he did each fall, if he would get a fair price for all his work. How quickly the year had passed. It was almost twelve months since he'd had the racket with Clements at Scanlan's. Then there'd been the meeting with Bob Sexton, the building of the crew, and the regatta. He wasn't going to any tavern on his own once he settled with the merchants this time. He wouldn't be alone, anyway. Tommy was going with him. The boy was nine now, and Kate's cooking had done him a world of good. He was healthy, and starting to sprout up like a weed.

He got some freshly cut hay for Prince, tossed it over the fence of the pound, and lingered to admire the horse. Prince trotted up and nibbled the hay, tossing his head up and down as if thanking John. John reached out and patted the sleek neck, then turned around and headed for the house.

"Kate! Tommy!" A low murmuring crept through the hall. It was coming from the parlour. John followed the sound.

"What are ye doing in here?" John said, looking at Tommy's head bent over a book. Kate was sitting beside him on the couch.

"Sure, I'm going to make my first communion soon. I'm learning the Catechism. Aunt Kate's helping me." Tommy looked at the ceiling and rolled his eyes. "I knows most all of it by heart now."

"I'm going to go out and cut some hay. I'll be back in a couple of hours, about suppertime."

Tommy moved closer to Kate and looked up at John. "Aunt Kate says you and her are going to adopt me. And then I'll be a Whelan just like you, won't I, Uncle John?"

Kate kissed the soft hair on the top of his head. John felt a lump rising in his throat. He coughed and then spoke. "Sure, you're already a Whelan, my son. We just got to tell the government about it."

"That's right," said Kate. "You're our son, and you'll be that forever. You can call us Mother and Father if you wants. But you don't have to." Kate looked away from him and took up her knitting.

"Forever?" Tommy smiled. "You mean till I grows up, Mother."

"Till you grows up and long after that, my child." Kate's voice was so full of joy John could hardly bear it.

A couple of hours of light remained to the day. John stood alone in the meadow. A second crop of hay was ripe. He was anxious to begin his favourite chore. First he had to make the scythe as sharp as a lance.

The sharpening stone slid across the edge of the scythe.

He touched the warm blade, then gripped the handle. The sunlight skimmed across the metal, making him blink as he began sweeping through the meadow. The grass fell easily, in snake-like patterns. He kept cutting until it was almost dark. Tommy was suddenly beside him, although he hadn't seen the boy approach.

"Finished me lessons and supper's ready, Father."

"Good. I'm famished." John picked up the sharpening stone and placed the scythe on his shoulder. He took Tommy's hand, and they headed home.

Author's Note

The writing of this story was long overdue: it's been 114 years since the members of the 1901 Outer Cove winning crew's record was set. Everyone I talked to when I first considered writing this book wondered why the story hadn't already been written. But it wasn't as easy as that; I had only a few pages of facts to work with at the beginning. I had plenty of passion about the St. John's Regatta, but passion comes from the heart. I needed to connect my heart to my mind to start the process of creating what the world of these fishermen might have been like in 1901. That required a lot of research and a lot of imagining. I went back to 1900 and started my yarn.

I've left a good chunk of my heart in this book, and, I hope, some insight into the hearts of those who have rowed on Quidi Vidi Lake and the hearts of tens of thousands who have followed "the races."

Acknowledgements

Many thanks to Paul Butler, the best teacher and mentor a writer could have.

My wife, Carol, is a saint for enduring my impatience while I was working on *A Stroke in Time*.

A debt of gratitude is owed to those who read the pre-publication manuscript. Their lovely words are on the cover and inside the book.

Special thanks to Paddy Hickey, Agnes Hickey, and Dave J. Hickey of Outer Cove, the Croke family and the late Pat Coady of Outer Cove, and the late Margaret Houlihan of Flatrock for sharing their stories.

Thanks to Martin Boland, whose three pages of facts of Regatta Day, 1901, were the fuel that really got me started.

Thanks to Dick Carroll, a great storyteller of the races who hasn't missed a regatta in eighty years.

I am eternally grateful to Andrea Roberts and Ray Walsh for helping me manage Word documents.

Thanks to all the great rowers, past and present, who inspired me to write about the sport.

I would like to extend my gratitude to Jessica Grant, Jean Simpson, and Michael Winter, writers-in-residence at Memorial University.

Thank you, Ed Kavanagh, for insisting on the many changes this book needed to make it better (which involved making me rewrite the whole darn manuscript).

I am also grateful to Susan Rendell for her gift of managing the words of this greenhorn writer.

Printed in Great Britain
by Amazon

49014208R00136